Jennifer Johnston is one of the foremost writers of her generation. Her many awards include the Whitbread Prize (*The Old Jest*), and the *Evening Standard* Best First Novel Award (*The Captains and the Kings*). She was also shortlisted for the Booker Prize with *Shadows on our Skin*.

Praise for Jennifer Johnston:

'Roddy Doyle has called her "the best writer in Ireland" and I'm not going to argue. Any novel by the great Johnston is an event . . . wisdom, pinpoint observation and elegance . . . even the surprises are surprising . . . richly satisfying' Kate Saunders, *The Times*

'Rich and disconcerting' *Financial Times*

'Irresistible' *Times Literary Supplement*

'Superbly executed . . . both enchanted and enchanting' *Daily Telegraph*

'A bittersweet demonstration of the impossibility of love . . . shot through with luminous magic' John Walsh, *Independent*

'Quiveringly tender and sensitive . . . as perfect and as minutely aware as ever' *Sunday Independent* (Ireland)

'An immaculate artist: understated, unshowy, a careful and economical craftswoman of language and all the loose, unwieldy stuff of emotion' *Scotsman*

'One of Ireland's finest writers' *Sunday Tribune*

'Johnston shows once again how well she understands human nature, its paradoxes, its strengths, cruelties and frailties' *Observer*

'Wonderful . . . funny and sad' *Daily Express*

'Jennife . . . her human nature'

Jennifer Johnston

Shadowstory

headline
review

First published in 2011 by HEADLINE REVIEW
An imprint of HEADLINE PUBLISHING GROUP

First published in paperback in 2012 by HEADLINE REVIEW
An imprint of HEADLINE PUBLISHING GROUP

I

Cataloguing in Publication Data is available from the British Library

ISBN 978 0 7553 8349 8

Typeset in Centaur by Avon DataSet Ltd,
Bidford-on-Avon, Warwickshire

Printed and bound in Great Britain by
Clays Ltd, St Ives plc

Headline's policy is to use papers that are natural, renewable and
recyclable products and made from wood grown in sustainable forests.
The logging and manufacturing processes are expected to conform
to the environmental regulations of the country of origin.

HEADLINE PUBLISHING GROUP
An Hachette UK Company
338 Euston Road
London NW1 3BH

www.headline.co.uk
www.hachette.co.uk

Pour Philippe

Sam was five years old when I was born.

He was my uncle.

My father had been twenty when Sam was born, to all intents and purposes a grown-up man. They had never had the chance to become close friends, more nodding acquaintances. There were three brothers and a sister between them, each one guarding my father from the youngest of the pack.

Nowadays people don't have six children, they don't have time or money to spend on six children, they don't have space to hide from them when it becomes necessary, which it does from time to time; to hide from their demands, their tears, their jokes, even their all-consuming love.

Anyway, the five-year-old Sam is supposed to have said, when brought in on day three of my life to see me in the nursing home, 'Why?' and turned reproachful eyes on my mother.

She laughed and snuggled herself more comfortably into her pile of pillows.

'What do you mean why, dear Sam? A baby is a baby. There are no whys about a baby. This is my baby, my dear little pretty Polly baby. My sweet little popsicle.' My mother was given to such outbursts, which used to embarrass the hell out of me in later years, but this time merely succeeded in causing a flood of tears that rose inside Sam and fell from his eyes like a great waterfall.

'Sam! Sweetheart. Why the tears? Don't cry, baby. Dear Sam. You are upsetting me. You mustn't upset people who've just had babies.' She put out her hand and stroked his hair. He continued to cry. After a little while she handed him a handkerchief. 'Mop up,' she said. 'Tell you what we'll do, we'll share her. You can be her special person. You could have been her godfather, but we won't be doing any of that stuff, so you can be her special person. How about that?'

He continued to cry.

'Oh God, Sam, do shut up. You're snivelling. Go and wash your face. You look snotty.'

Sam wailed. She gave him a friendly push.

'Go, Sammy, go on. You'll wake the baby and she'll cry and then I'll cry. The room will be full of bawling people. Out in the corridor they'll start and soon the whole nursing home will be awash. Warm tears rolling down the stairs and whose fault? Whose fault, Sammy boy? Hey.' And Sammy lifted up his face and laughed.

That was our first meeting, and I, wrapped and swaddled and tucked like an expensive parcel, slept through all those important moments.

At my grandparents' house, which was quite far away from where we lived in Dublin, near the blue turbulent ocean, they had a tennis court; a good, expensive one made of orange clay. You could hear the relentless sea as you sat by the court watching or thinking your own thoughts and smell the salt in the air. The court was surrounded by a high wire fence over which Sam and his siblings or school friends used to belt tennis balls when they were not playing very seriously. A shout would go up: 'Baby. Go fetch,' and this willing fool would run out through the gate in the fence and begin hunting in the shrubby undergrowth. Sometimes you found much more interesting things than tennis balls in that undergrowth: a silver sixpence carrying on it the head of George V, *D.G. Rex F.D. Imp* still readable. 1934, six years before I was born. I brought it into the house and showed it to my grandma. She examined it with care.

'Well aren't you the lucky little one,' she said, handing it back to me. 'You'll be able to buy lots of ice cream with that. Don't lose it. Finders keepers, losers weepers. We don't want you weeping, do we?'

'What do those words mean? Imp is the only one I know. Is he an imp?' I pointed to the bearded man on the coin.

She laughed. 'No, dear Polly. He was the king of England. He's dead now and if you examine any other coins that may come your way, you'll see a totally different face. Maybe a beardless face or even an old woman's. He isn't an imp either . . . an imp, my darling, is a bad brat of a fairy, always up to no good, like some imps around here. This imp is short for the Latin word that means emperor. Imperator.'

'Imperator.' I got my tongue round the wonderful word. 'Is an emperor important?'

'I suppose so. They sort of hold things together. Julius Caesar was one, and Napoleon, and then there was the Holy Roman Emperor and—'

'Jesus,' I said helpfully.

She shook her head. 'No, darling. He was never an emperor. He was just a man. A plain and simple man.'

Over the years I found many treasures amongst the long grass and the bushes there, to the left of the tennis court, with the ocean stirring and murmuring not too far away: a sheep's skull, white and shiny, flat on top with quite a few teeth still intact; Grandma didn't like it much. She flicked it with a finger and said, 'Not too many brains would have fitted in there. Not a house object, Polly darling, keep it outside somewhere.'

What else?

An old flatiron, heavy and rusted a sort of flaky orangey-brown colour. This I just threw further away into the deeper, darker grass, under the tall oak trees.

There is a story to tell about those oak trees; there are fifty-seven of them, or rather there were at that time. God knows what has happened to the beauties since I last saw them years ago. My many-times-grandfather had in 1802 married a young woman from County Down who had brought with her as a part of her dowry a hundred acorns in a small sack. This grove of oaks, almost a forest one might say, to the left side of the tennis court and covering a small hill, had grown from those acorns, and according to Grandma was one of the wonders of Ireland. But, I learnt as I grew older, you couldn't always believe everything that Grandma told you. She was a great one for tall tales.

'Beatrice is off again, down some little avenue of her own invention,' Grandpa would say, sometimes fondly, sometimes with a little hint of irritation in his voice. When he became irritated he would bang with his stick on the floor — rat tat rattat — and his dog Pluto would thump with his tail and give a little warning growl, nothing else, just a low throaty growl, which meant: I'm with the boss. Let ye all take care.

He never left Grandpa's side. At night, he slept on a rug beside the old man's bed, and each day they would go walking up and down around the place, discussing with the men the whys and wherefores of the way things were being done, and checking the crops, the cattle, the height of the river, the holes to be mended in the long stone walls, and when Grandpa bicycled into Kinvara or to visit friends Pluto galloped beside him. That was a sight to see, the tall, thin old man and the rough-haired wolfhound hard at it along the back roads of County Galway and County Clare. Grandpa was a taciturn man, given to grunts and words of one syllable, never bad-tempered, merely a man of silence. He smiled when amused, rather than laughed. He loved my grand-mother deeply and would touch her whenever the opportunity arose, running his fingers up her arm, or pushing his hand in underneath the heavy bun at the back of her head and stroking her warm neck; he would take her fingers and kiss them sometimes, one at a time, and then drop her hand as if embarrassed by this gentle act.

His left leg was the bad one; it seemed several inches shorter than the right one. He walked always with a stick, propelling himself along at great speed, but in an ungainly fashion. He never swam or wore shorts, so I have no idea what his leg looked like, but I presume it was what he considered to be unattractive and it was his vanity that made him keep it covered.

'Grandpa.' I would have been five or six. I don't remember where the conversation took place, but I remember the words, his face, and the sound his stick made tapping on the ground.

'So, Baby, what is it you want to know today?'

'What is the matter with your leg?'

He frowned. He scratched the corner of his left eye. He tapped his stick on the floor. I didn't think that he was going to answer me and then suddenly he did.

'In nineteen hundred and seventeen, near a river called the Somme, I had an altercation with a shell. Not your normal thing you pick up on the beach and bring home to show your grandmother, but a metal object, an instrument of war. An altercation. You can look up that word in the dictionary and you can find the river Somme in an atlas. I was one of the lucky ones; almost all the men with me were blown to bloody flitters.' He shut his mouth tight and gestured with a hand that I should leave him. I crept away, very conscious that I had made some awful blunder in bringing up the subject.

I found out what altercation meant quite quickly; it took me longer to find out where the Somme was. He hadn't mentioned France.

* * *

Ever since the earliest days of my remembering I had spent a lot of my life at Kildarragh. The next war was on; that was why.

My father, whose career had been gathering momentum at the Bar, had thrown it up and without telling anyone where he was going had nipped on to the Mail Boat, gone to England and joined the Irish Guards.

He had telephoned my mother from London and told her and she had cried, so she told me years later.

'You'll tell them at Kildarragh for me, won't you?'

'No. I won't. You must do your own dirty work.'

'Nonie . . . please.'

'No. Isn't it enough that you've left me here having your baby and gone off playing at soldiers, but I have to tell your parents? No. I won't. Your father'll have a fit.'

'No he won't. He knows it's not like the last one. Hitler is a truly wicked man and has to be stopped and I bet Ireland will join in and then I'll come back and join our own army. Come on, darling, please. Be kind. I can't get home and I don't want to say this in a letter or on the bloody telephone. You go down and tell them about the baby and then about this.'

She cried but of course she did as he had asked and the reaction was just as she had feared; Grandpa said no word, but limped off up the stairs to his library, a room above the porch, which he called his holy of holies. I asked him once what he did in there and he answered me, 'I read, Baby and I think, both activities for which you need silence.' After Nonie's news he hadn't come out for three days, except to go to the kitchen in the middle of the night, where Sadie, the cook, who knew the ropes, left food out for him.

'Do ye want the poor man to starve to death?' she had said to my mother. 'Of course I leave food for him whenever he gets in one of his little stews. You wouldn't want the poor man to fade away before he sees his lovely little grandchild. His first grandchild.' No one ever seemed to tell Sadie anything of importance, but she always knew everything that was going on. She knew for instance that Harry would be the next to go and the morning when he put his foot on the step at the back of the trap and was about to spring in she came running out of the hall door with a parcel in her hands. She pushed past Grandma and Grandpa, who were standing in silence on the steps, and thrust the parcel into Harry's hands. 'It's for you. I baked it for you and if you see Greg you can give him some. If you see him. It's a good real rich fruit cake, with . . . with Guinness, and some of the master's port. I knew this would happen. I knew. But this will keep up your spirits. Yes.'

He stepped carefully down from the trap on to the gravel and put his arms around her.

'Dear Sadie.' His voice was gritty. 'I love you so much, and so does Greg. We all do.'

'Why do you go, so, to this horrible war? It's not your war, child dear, and you're breaking their hearts, and mine too.'

'It's everyone's war. But we'll be safely back before too long. Mind them for me, Sadie. Feed them well. Love them well. Greg and I will mind each other.' He kissed her cheek and jumped back into the trap and rattled away off down the avenue with the paper parcel gripped tightly on his knees.

My mother told me these little pieces of conversation years later and each piece of life that she unfolded for me I wrote down in a little notebook, trying as best I could to remember her very words.

My mother went to England, to be near my father, when I was about nine months old and I was sent to live at Kildarragh. As my father was, at that stage, in North Africa, she might as well have remained at home, because when he did get leave they both came home and played with me on the shore or in the garden, ate copiously, slept a lot and then disappeared again. There are albums full of snapshots of them and me and Sam, Jassie, Mickey and Patrick, all seeming to be very happy. Buckets and spades, wet towels, tennis racquets, golf clubs and horses are the props that surround us in those pictures. I remember nothing; only when I look at the pictures do I say to myself, yes, it must have been like that.

Jassie went back with Greg and Nonie the last time. She had just finished in Trinity, sailed through and come out with a first in history, which triumph she celebrated by announcing at dinner that she was going to England with Greg to join the WAAF. My mother told me that total silence fell at the table. After a long time Grandpa stood up slowly and walked across the room to the door, with Pluto beside him. He turned.

'I don't understand what you're up to at all.'

He left the room.

He didn't appear again until after they had gone the next morning; my mother said that she saw him at the window of his library, hand upraised in farewell or perhaps blessing as they trotted down the avenue in the trap.

That was 1944 and I never saw my father again. I have in my head an imaginary picture of how he died, debonair; I like to think of him like that, truly debonair, as they tell me he had been on the hunting field, being driven through a small village that had just been liberated, his tin hat beside him on the seat. I feel sure he was singing and a sniper from an upstairs window caught him in mid-note, right in the head. His driver stamped on the accelerator and drove him to the nearest field hospital, but that burst of speed was unnecessary: he had been killed when the bullet entered his skull. He is out there now in one of those neat graveyards in Normandy, tended and nurtured by caring people and surrounded by his pals, or should I say comrades? I have never been to see his grave, nor will I ever go. I feel as my grandfather did about war and killing; we have to find some other way to overcome tyrants.

Anyway, Jassie was killed in London by a flying bomb in the spring of 1945, when the war was almost over; another few weeks and she would have survived as Harry had and come home to get on with real life. Her name and my father's are written on a granite stone in the little graveyard that surrounds the parish church.

In loving memory of Greg and Jassie who gave their lives
so that the world might be a better place.

That is what the words say.

'Nothing else, thank you, rector. That covers everything. No battle honours, no God, no Jesus Christ. Just those plain words. I know your intentions are good, rector, but that will do.' Grandma sighed, but said nothing as Grandpa spoke. I was five, able to remember things, to see things and imprint them on my mind, to hear things and carry the words with me.

I lived then for most of the time with my mother in a small house in Sandymount. We were as close to the sea as you could get. A narrow path ran between our hall door and the gate on to the road; across the road was a low wall, then a stretch of unkempt grass where boys played football every evening, then another wall and then a drop down on to the shore. The sea at high tide came right up to that drop and when the weather was stormy and the wind blew from the north it would crash over the wall, and the grass and the road, and the waves would lick at our gate, sometimes even sneaking through, trying to reach our hall door. My mother wouldn't let me out of the house on my own on such stormy days; she said I might get blown away. I used to look at the seagulls being tossed around in the sky and think that I might enjoy that, but she was adamant. The blue sea, the grey sea, sometimes almost black, the green sea, the sparkling sea, the calm dull sea, smooth as silk, daytime night-time, in and out it came and went in huge looping movements over the corrugated sand. So far it went out some days that you could not see even a breath of it between Sandymount and the hill of Howth. And the ships steaming in and out of the port seemed to float on air. I used to stand on the cross bar of our gate and look across the street and the two walls at the changing sea and the wide bay and the evening sunlight flashing in the windows of the houses on the hill of Howth and I was happy. I remember that happiness.

* * *

My mother, of course, being young and resilient, began to see and be seen with other men. She was not only intelligent and funny, but there was also some aura of glamour that was draped around her shoulders like a dim shawl. Everyone wanted to make her happy.

At that time we had a little rackety car; my father had owned it before the war and it had sat through all those years on bricks in a shed at Kildarragh. Almost the first thing that Harry had done when he came home after the war was to take out the car and fiddle with it, clean it up, fix the roof which was a little dilapidated, put new tyres on the wheels, pinch some of his father's carefully hoarded petrol and drive it up to Dublin. He arrived at our gate and blew the horn.

My mother opened the door and looked out.

'Eureka,' he shouted.

I had never heard the word before; it echoed round

my head, it hit the low wall on the other side of the street and came back to me as I peered out from behind my mother.

Eureka.

'Darling Harry. Poll, sweetheart, it's Harry.'

Eureka.

She ran down the path and they met at the gate and hugged each other.

'How lovely to see you. How well you look, how unmilitary. Have you come up to paint the town red?'

He laughed. 'No. I came to see you and Baby. Come on, Baby, give us a kiss.'

I remained at the hall door, still tussling with the word and with his unfamiliarity.

Eureka.

'She's going through a shy phase. Pay no attention to her and she'll sort herself out. And you have wheels.'

'You have wheels. I've fixed it up for you. It's Greg's. Don't you remember it? Of course you do. Hop in. Hop in, Baby. I'll take you both for a spin.'

Eureka meant magic.

I ran down the path and clambered into the back of the car. Magic, I thought, this is magic. This is eureka.

We are going to spin in this small black car. I knew about spinning. I can spin.

Nonie was laughing, delighted, as she got in.

'My car. You are a wonder, Harry. Let's go to the top of Bray head. Will she go up that hill? What do you think?'

'Of course she will.' And we drove off, leaving the gate and the hall door open, a thing we did often in those innocent post-war days.

* * *

I spent more and more of my time at Kildarragh; when my school terms ended Nonie would dump me and my suitcase in the baby Austin and off we would go.

'It's good for you, all that fresh air, and you love Sam, don't you? Sam is your favourite person, isn't he? I have to get some sun. I can't live without my ration of sun. This poor old island of ours doesn't get enough to do me and anyway, darling Polly, you love Kildarragh and the family.' So she would burble on and I would sit in the front seat and not say a word. Yes, she was right, I did love Kildarragh, but what I really wanted and wished for was that she and I would both go and live there for ever, even in the back yard where the horses were; we could fit neatly into a few rooms there and not bother anyone and hear the snorts and rattles from the horses' stalls and I could have a dog of my own, not just share Pluto with Grandpa. But then I would think to myself, as we joggled across Ireland, I would miss the bay, and the wrinkled sand and the ships floating past the hill of Howth, and sometimes I would fall asleep and be woken for lunch and a pee in Ballinasloe.

'The one thing I don't like about being here,' I said to Grandma, as we stood on the steps, having waved goodbye to Nonie.

'What's that, darling? I do hope it's nothing too serious.'

'Everyone here calls me Baby. I'm not a baby. I'm almost seven.'

'Oh, darling, that is so serious. I will do something about it at once.' She touched my shoulder and went into the house.

POLLY IS NO LONGER A BABY. SHE IS ALMOST SEVEN. PLEASE REMEMBER THIS.

WHEN YOU ARE ADDRESSING THE
YOUNGEST MEMBER OF THIS FAMILY
PLEASE REMEMBER THAT HER NAME
IS POLLY.

THERE ARE NO BABIES IN THIS HOUSE
ANY MORE.

Such messages littered the place, written in large black or red letters; they lay on tables, were stuck to doors, were tucked into the frames of mirrors: you couldn't miss them. Only Sam continued to call me Baby.

It must have been about that time that I was given the fat pony, chestnut with a long black mane and eyelashes, I kid you not, thick, thick eyelashes, which he used like a cocotte. His name was Benjy and he and I joined Grandpa and Pluto for their morning walk each day; hail, rain or snow the four of us would set off down the avenue. Grandpa knew each corner in the road, each blade of grass it seemed. Each desolate and tumbled cottage had its story and he knew them all and soon I knew most of them too; sometimes we would go down to the beach and he would thump with his stick and shout, 'Go, Benjy, go. Gallop.' And off we would go, through the edge of the sea, tossing up sparkles of silver behind us as we galloped, and Pluto ran beside us, his pink tongue lolling from his mouth.

When we reached the high rocks at the far end of the beach we would stop for a few minutes of quiet breathing and then trot in a dignified way back to where Grandpa would be standing waiting, staring out towards America, or anyway that's what he told me when I asked him.

'America. That's where they've all gone, Polly. The land of opportunity. Maybe I should have gone myself. I'd be a rich old man out there, with two legs instead of only one and a half. And central heating in my house.'

'You wouldn't have me.'

He laughed. 'True. Too true, and where would I be without you, Baby dear?'

'Polly.'

'Do excuse me, Polly. I am becoming a forgetful old man. Home. Hey, Pluto. Benjy. Polly, home.'

'What do you and Dad talk about when you go for your walks?' Sam asked me later on that same holiday. We were sitting on top of a haystack in the field below the house. The sun was shining and the hay was prickling my legs.

'He tells me stories.'

'Truth or fiction?'

'What's fiction?'

'Makey-uppy. Like you read in books.'

'Oh no. I think they're truth. About people who used to live here. People who went to America and became rich.'

'Sounds like fiction to me.'

'People who have central heating in their houses.'

'Oh, for God's sake!'

'He'd like that. Do you think he misses Jassie?'

'We all miss Jassie.'

'I think that's why he takes me out with him. Perhaps he's pretending that I'm Jassie.'

'Jassie was grown up. You're just a baby yet.'

'I am not. I'm seven. That's not a baby. Grandma said that seven wasn't a baby.'

'You don't stay up for dinner. You read baby books like *Winnie-the-Pooh*, you ride a fat little pony that can only go at two miles an hour. And I bet you don't know what fuck means.'

'That's a rude word. We're not allowed to say it.' I

could feel the tears rising up inside me. I pinched the inside of my arm, but they kept on rising.

'You're a fucky little baby. Crybaby. I can see you crying. Fuck, fucky, fucky.'

I put my hands over my ears and buried my head in the hay. It was hot, but smelled sweet; it scratched at my face. I stayed there for what seemed like ages and ages and when I peeped out he was lying on his back staring up at the blue sky. He was smiling.

'I know something about Nonie that you don't.'

'I bet you don't. I bet I know everything about her. More than you do anyway.'

'I heard Mum and Dad talking last night . . .'

'You listened . . .'

'I was passing the door and I heard . . . I only listened for a moment, but I heard . . . Nonie is going to get married. You're going to have a new father.'

I threw myself at him, screaming and slapping at his face. He just lay there and laughed; he didn't seem to mind the slaps which were stinging my fingers. It seemed pointless, so I stopped and I lay there in the hay, my eyes blinded with tears, the whole world around me in shreds.

'It's not true, 'I said at last. 'Not not true. I don't want a new father. I want my own father back. She would have told me. She wouldn't have told anyone else. She would not . . .' I turned over on to my stomach and bit the side of his leg. 'I hate you. You are a horrid teasing fuck boy.'

He kicked at me with his foot and I slid down the side of the haystack and ran towards the house.

There were five steps up to the hall door, which stood open in the daytime, winter and summer, and led into a long glass-fronted porch, held up by tall granite columns and filled with stone urns of all designs and decorations in which grew in great profusion flowering plants and shrubs, azaleas, camellias, sweet-smelling geraniums, even, if my memory serves me right, two rhododendrons with ruby red flowers like huge bells; the smell when you entered over-whelmed you with its richness. Grandma called it her winter garden, which made Grandpa laugh. *'Folie de grandeur,'* he would snort and she would slap him on the arm.

I started to boohoo and sniffle when I came in sight of the house; no point I thought in creating a fuss with no one around to hear me. Grandma came running out of the door, secateurs in hand.

'Polly, darling. Polly. What's the matter? Why such terrible sadness? Did you fall, darling?' She almost jumped down the steps and pulled me into her arms. 'There,' she said. 'There there, my darling baby.'

She took a handkerchief from her pocket and wiped my face. We walked up the steps together and she pushed me down on to one of the wrought-iron seats that were there amongst the plants. She sat down beside me.

'Now. What's all this about?'

'Sam said . . . that Mummy was going to be married. That I was going to have a new father.' The tears poured out again, unstoppable.

She put an arm around my shoulders. 'Bloody Sam,' was all she said for quite a long time. Then she patted my arm.

'Come,' she said briskly. 'We'll go and see Grandpa. You must wash your face first. He'd have a fit if he saw you looking like that.'

I was obedient as a lamb. I let her take me to the cloakroom and wipe my face and hands with warm soapy water. I looked at myself in the mirror above the basin and thought how ugly I looked, red, bleary, smeared with snot. The flannel smoothed my face, and calmed the inside of my head.

'I bit him.'

I don't know why I felt like telling her this; I suppose something inside me said it was better that I should tell her than that Sam should. She sighed and picked up the towel and began to pat my face dry.

'That was a silly thing to do. No matter what he said. It would be a pity if we all started to call you Baby again. Only babies bite, you know. And untrained animals. So try to keep your teeth under control, Polly dear. In future, when you are provoked, do try your hardest. There, you look better now.' She patted my hair this way and that for a moment. 'I know how provoking he can be.' We walked across the big stone-flagged hall. Above us, halfway up the stairs a stained glass window cast red and blue patterns down the stairs. When we reached the door of his library she stopped and muttered in a low voice, 'We won't mention the biting. OK?' I nodded and we went in. He was sitting in his high-backed arm chair, his head drooping down towards a book that he held in his hands; beside him on the floor Pluto lay stretched, his tail rhythmically beating on the floor in welcome.

'Ha,' said Grandpa. 'Ha. Yes, ladies. Do come in.' He threw his book down on to the floor beside him. 'To what do I owe the honour?'

Grandma took my hand in hers and squeezed it tightly.

'That bad boy, that villainous brat of a boy, has told Polly . . . you know. He listens at doors. I've always known that, I mean to say who doesn't if given the opportunity, but he's told her . . . you know, that which he shouldn't.'

The old man's hand banged down on the table in front of him. 'About Nonie?'

'What else is there to tell?'

He turned to me and smiled. 'Well now, little Polly, you know. Your mother would have told you when she came to fetch you, but now you know.' He cleared his throat. He put out a hand and touched my hair, his fingers softly stroking the knotted ringlets that fell down past my face. I would cut them off, I thought to myself, that would show her, that would serve her right; she loved brushing and combing my hair, she loved the silkiness of it, she loved twisting it round her fingers into long soft curls. I would show her. I became aware that they were both standing quite still staring at me, his hand still on my head.

'I don't care. I never loved her best anyway.' I heard the words coming out of my mouth.

We all stood in silence.

'I think,' said Grandma, after a while, 'that we'll have a cup of tea and drop scones. In the kitchen. I do believe that Sadie has just made drop scones.' She took my hand in hers. 'And raspberry jam.' She gently pulled me towards the door. 'You can have sugar in your tea, if you want it. I found some pre-war lumps the other day in the back of a cupboard in the pantry.'

'And send that rapscallion to me when he comes in,' Grandfather said as we closed the door. 'I'll give him what for.'

The passage to the kitchen was long and dark, lined with neatly stacked logs and baskets of turf and kindling. From time to time a mouse would run across the flagstones, darting just ahead of your feet, was it a shadow, a blown leaf or a mouse, it was impossible to tell. Sadie kept the heavy kitchen door closed.

'I don't want them things scampering round in my kitchen. Let them stay out there with the sticks. Dirty objects.' So she and the cats ruled over a mouse-free kitchen. It was also warm and murmuring.

'Little Baby.' She looked at me with sympathy as we came in. 'Let you sit now in Sadie's chair.' She scooped an orange cat off the big basket chair and pushed it an inch nearer to the range. 'The drop scones are just this minute off the griddle. Let you sit, little Baby, and Lily can sleep in peace on your knee. There's nothing like a cat on your knee for giving you comfort.' She arranged me among the cushions and put the cat on my knee. Lily opened one eye and looked into my face and then returned to her sleep. From time to time she purred for a while and I could feel the trembling of her warm body through my legs.

'Did I not say to you before that that lad knows too much? He listens. Haven't I seen him with my own two eyes walking slowly past a door, his ears pricked like an eager dog? He knows more than is good for him and he won't keep it to himself. Not a bit of it. Teasing, throwing out bits of information here and there, there's no harm in his head, it's just teasing.'

Grandma was buttering drop scones and nodding her head in time to Sadie's voice. Sadie scolded on, but it wasn't real scolding, I knew that. She loved Sam, she loved the fact that given his age he probably knew as much about what was going on around the place as she did. She, too, was a listener and a watcher; not a soul arrived on the front doorstep without Sadie knowing who they were and what it was they wanted.

'Just a word or two of strictness from the master'll put him in the right direction. Not a shout mind you, just a quiet and reasonable word. Wouldn't you say?'

Grandma scooped a spoonful of raspberry jam on to a scone and came across the room and handed it to me.

'Would you like to say that to him . . . to the master?'

'Doesn't he always listen to you, missus dear. Every word that drops from your lips is like the blessed gospel.'

Grandma laughed.

The drop scone was delicious, warm and buttery, and the jam was wonderful. I needed another one. Sadie was pouring boiling water from the kettle into a large brown teapot. Grandma was laughing. The sunlight came in through the window in great warm stripes. My eyes blinked with sleepiness. The cat on my knee purred.

'Prehaps,' I said, it might have been hours later. The two women were sitting, old friends at the table, their cups pushed aside. Clouds had covered the sun and we were in a grey darkness. They turned and looked at me as I spoke. 'Prehaps I could come and live here with you. Not just stay . . . live for ever.'

'What a lovely thought, Polly dear. We would love nothing more, but you must think about your poor mother. She wouldn't like that at all. She would be bereft.'

'She will be married again. She'll have a husband.'

'That's not the same as your own daughter. Not at all the same. She couldn't live without you. Could she, Sadie?'

Sadie shook her head. Words seemed to have abandoned her.

'You see, darling, Nonie's a young woman. You wouldn't want her to be growing old and lonely. That's sad. This way she will have someone with her always. Like me and Grandpa.'

'She will have me.'

'No. You'll grow up and leave home. That's the way of things. You'll want to see the world, get married, have children of your own. To grow old on your own is hard.'

'You never said a truer word,' said Sadie. She stood up and collected the debris from the table. 'Back to work or ye'll get no dinner. Baby can stay there if she wants. She looks cosy. Snug as a bug in a rug.' She handed me another drop scone and I lay curled in her chair with the cat asleep on my knee.

*   *   *

When Nonie came to collect me she was married. She wore a different gold ring on her finger and her gaiety was almost manic. She held me to her in hug after breathless hug.

'Poll darling, darling. I've got such news to tell you. Wonderful, wonderful news.'

'You're married.'

She let go of me and looked reproachfully at Grandma and Grandpa. 'How could—'

Grandma put up her hand. 'I promise you it wasn't

us. We never breathed a word. It was a little bird told her. These secrets are hard to keep.'

'What little bird?'

'Never you mind. Just a little bird. We won't talk about it any more. Let us have a drink and celebrate.'

'What's his name?' I asked my mother.

'Didn't the little bird tell you that?'

I felt Grandpa's hand on my shoulder.

'Don't be angry with the child, Nonie. We're all delighted that you're happy, but you should have told Baby. Of course you should. She is the most important person in your life. You are the most important person in hers. You've made her unhappy. Now you must tell her how sorry you are to have done that. How mistaken you were to treat her like an infant. And you must remember in future that secrets have wings . . . like little birds.'

My mother stood for a moment looking down at the floor, then she took a step towards me and falling to her knees put her arms around me.

'Polly, Polly, darling Poll. I am soooooo sorry. I am an abominable person. You are the most important person in my life. Forgive me. It's Charles. I got married to Charles. You like him, I know. And he loves you. And we're all going to be happy. I promise you that.'

I looked up and saw Grandpa's face gravely nodding at me, so I allowed myself to be swept away in my mother's embrace. I allowed her warm tears to wash over me. I allowed her warm words to drip through my ears and enter into my whole body. I was so full of her love that I felt nothing else, no sorrow, no anger, just a wonderful dream of happiness.

They even let me drink a mouthful of champagne and when I sneezed we all laughed. Even Pluto grinned and thumped my legs with his tail.

*　*　*

At the end of that summer Sam went to school in England. Grandma went over with him on the Mail Boat and she came to see us in Sandymount on her way back to Kildarragh. She looked old and tired when she arrived with us about eight o'clock in the morning. I stared at her. I had never seen her looking old before, or dishevelled, and I was wondering if it was because she was in our house in Dublin rather than in her own home. Could a place have that sort of effect on you?

'He cried,' I heard her say, 'and at that moment I almost brought him home with me. But I thought how cross his father would be when we both trailed in through the door.' She gave a sad little sniff and her voice trembled. 'None of the others ever cried.'

'Sam wouldn't cry,' I said. 'Sam never cries. Sam is brave as a lion.'

'Eat your porridge, Polly, or you'll be late for school.' That was my mother, sounding cross. She leant over the table and put her hand on Grandma's arm. 'Darling Beatrice, don't fret. He'll be fine. He was trying it on.'

Grandma shook her head, her hair dancing around her face. 'No. He was crying. Please don't go, he said. Please don't leave me here. Please, Ma. I ran. I had to run or I would have pulled him along with me.'

At this moment Charles got up from the table. 'Come along, Polly, you'll be late for school.'

I wanted to stay, to hear the rest, but his voice sounded as if I had no hope, so I got up. I kissed Mother and I kissed Grandma, who put her hands on my shoulders and held me for a moment. Then I went to school and when I came back in the afternoon she had gone, all the way back to Kildarragh and Grandpa.

'Where's Grandma?'

'She's gone back home. She had a little sleep and then she got the afternoon train.'

'All on her own?'

'Yes, darling. Why not?'

'But . . .'

'But me no buts, Poll, she was fine. She was just tired from the journey.'

'She'll cry on the train.'

I had a horrible picture of her in my head sitting very upright in her seat with the countryside flashing past her and her face wet with tears. The other passengers would read their books and pretend not to notice.

'Don't be silly, darling, of course she won't. She'll be fine, right as rain.'

'I don't want to go to boarding school.'

She laughed. 'No problems there, my darling. We wouldn't dream of sending you away to school. Grandma and Grandpa are very old-fashioned when it comes to that sort of thing. We promise you, no boarding school.'

She told the truth. I was never sent away from home as Sam had been; instead she and Charles had two children, Sue and Shane, and I became the odd one out in my own family.

I went to Kildarragh still for part of every holiday, but couldn't help feeling each time I left Sandymount that I was leaving behind a unit in which I had no place. In photographs of us all I was always a step or two to the left or right, a slightly anxious smile on my face, looking like a polite visitor. I was hurt and jealous at the amount of time and attention that Nonie gave to Charles and then, when they arrived, to the babies, time and attention that I felt should surely have been spent on me. Even in Kildarragh things seemed to have changed: Sam had become monosyllabic and never seemed pleased to see me when I arrived. He no longer kissed me or pulled my hair, didn't want me shadowing him wherever he went, didn't want to come to the beach with me to swim. To him I was Baby still and who wanted to play with a baby? Grandma was sympathetic but unable to help.

'We all love you to bits, darling Polly. I can see you're having a difficult time, but everything will smooth itself out in the end. Don't mope and moon, dear child. If you want to bring a friend down here the next time you come, that's all right with me. Someone of your own age. Someone you can play with, a companion.' Of course I never did.

With Sam sulking and skulking around, the atmosphere of the place had changed. Patrick and Mickey had drifted off to Dublin and seldom came home and Harry lived in a cottage on the estate and was working hard learning how to keep everyone's head above water. He used to stay with us whenever he came up to Dublin, but we seldom saw the other two boys at all. Grandpa and Pluto were showing signs of old age; they walked more slowly and not so far, and on wet or very blowy days they barely put their noses out of the house. Grandpa read; parcels of books ordered from Hodges Figgis in Dublin arrived for him regularly. Eamon, the postman, would poke around in his sack and come up with the well-wrapped parcel.

'Books for the general,' he would say, handing them to me. 'He must have near every book in the wide world read by now.' 'And then he would pedal off round the back to have a cup of tea with Sadie.

'Why does he call Grandpa the general?'

'I've often wondered that myself,' said Grandma,

dipping her ginger biscuit in her eleven o'clock cup of coffee. 'It's probably respect of some sort, or misinformation maybe. I've been tempted to ask him, but I always feel he might be upset if I did. I wouldn't want to embarrass him.'

'Why would he be embarrassed?'

'Well, he just might be. You never can tell with people.'

'Does Grandpa know that some people call him General?'

She shook her head. 'Heavens, no. He'd be most upset. So don't you go telling him.'

'Why?'

'He doesn't like wars or fighting or armies.'

'Is that because he got his leg blown off by a shell?'

'No, ducky. He's never liked them. Now run off and play and don't be such a curiosity cat. You're giving me a little pain in my head.'

'I have no one to play with.'

'Saddle Benjy and go for a ride. He's getting too fat these days. He needs exercise. So do you. Run. Scoot.'

* * *

From time to time Sam would have a school friend to stay, sometimes two. They would ride off at about ten thirty in the morning with their togs and their sandwiches over their shoulders in canvas bags and arrive home about five thirty, sandy, dishevelled and full of bursting laughter and talk. When Grandpa heard their voices in the yard, he would throw open the window of his room and lean out over the sill to call down to the boys below. 'Look to your horses, boys. Horses come first.' 'Yes sir,' they would shout back to him, and set about the business of seeing their horses watered and comfortably ensconced in their boxes and the bridles and saddles tidied away to their places in the tack room ready for the next day's outing.

'If I didn't shout at them,' he said to me once as I stood beside him at the window, 'they'd just leave the beasts there, abandon them on the cobblestones for one of the men to see to. I know boys. Lazy little buggers. Yes, Pluto?' Pluto wagged his tail in agreement.

Some days they just stayed around the place and played vicious and interminable games of tennis which mainly consisted of hitting the ball very hard at their opponent's body or high over the wire, when up would go the cry of 'Baaaby' in their squeaky rough voices and I would pretend not to hear.

'She's not your sister, is she?' I heard one of them ask Sam one day.

'God, no. My niece.'

'Does she live here?'

'No. In Dublin. My brother was killed in the war. His wife married again. So a lot of Polly's life is filled with people who don't really belong to her. She prefers it here. She's just a kid.'

I squirmed. I kept out of their way.

And then there was that day that I clearly remember.

We were picking raspberries. Grandma always insisted that the fruit and vegetables had to be picked and brought to Sadie in the kitchen before any of us were allowed to embark on whatever plan might be in our heads for the rest of the day. Anyway, this morning we were shoulder high in the raspberry canes, being driven demented by midges and by the almost Mediterranean heat of the sun pressing down on our heads.

'Baby.'

I did not answer. I was twelve. I did not answer to Baby.

'Polly.' It was Sam's friend Marcus who called me this time.

'Yes?'

'We thought we might go rowing in Mr Maher's boat. Do you want to come?'

I looked at Sam. 'Why?'

'It might be cooler on the water.'

'No. Not why do you want to go rowing, why do you want me to come too?'

'We just do. We've been talking about you. We thought perhaps you might be a bit lonely. Sadie's packed some lunch for you too. Do come, Babe. Maher has told us we can use his outboard. It'll be fun.'

'Please come,' said Marcus.

'You've been talking about me?'

'Earlier this morning. Sam told me that your father was killed in the war. Mine was too. That's all. I thought you might be lonely.' He had a nice smile.

'Yes,' I said. 'I'd like to come.'

'We'll bring the raspberries to Sadie,' said Sam. 'You run up and get your togs and we'll meet you at the bike shed in ten minutes.'

We bicycled down to the little pier where Mr Maher

kept his boat and piled ourselves and our accoutrements in: towels, togs, a wicker basket covered with a white napkin, fishing lines, jumpers just in case.

'In case of what?' Marcus asked, gazing up at the blue sky.

'You never can tell,' muttered Sam. 'Untie that rope and jump in.'

He pushed us off, out through the rocks and the waving green weed and the flashing silver of the tiny fishes that darted under the bow, out past the buoys that marked where Mr Maher's lobster pots hung, and out past the long flat rock where two seals lay sunning themselves; they barely lifted their heads to watch us pass. The sea was like glass, in which was reflected the blue sky and the occasional bird that drifted on some air current, wings outstretched, with no destination in mind. And, of course, us. We perfect human beings leaned over the side of the boat and stared at our rippling faces in the water, and the sun made a bright path across the sea, and it has remained in my head as one of the best days of my life.

We discovered a small sandy cove where the trees formed a semicircle at the top of a gentle slope and the sand was golden and warm; we swam naked time and time again until our bodies were encrusted with salt and little sparkles of golden sand which clung to our arms and legs. We were eating strawberries when Marcus spoke.

'It's so splendidly pagan. We're gold. How do you paint gold? Everything is gold.' Strawberry juice dribbled over his chin as he talked. In the distance a cow bellowed.

He was right, everything was gold; the sun seemed to be loitering towards the west, a huge burning ball.

'Why do you want to paint it? It will be in my head for ever. I don't need to paint it.'

He shook his head. 'Things fade. I have to look at pictures of my father now, if I want to remember what he looked like. If he came out from behind that tree now, this moment, I probably wouldn't recognise him. I think I know what he would look like. But I think it is my imagination rather than any reality.'

The cow bellowed again and I felt sad rather than happy. It was if a cloud had come between me and the sun.

'Do you paint? Have you been painting while you've been here?'

'Yes, I paint. I'm going to art college in the autumn. Maybe there I can learn how to paint gold. Klimt painted gold. I adore Klimt.'

'You think you might become a painter? Live by being a painter?'

'I'd like to give it a shot.' He took another strawberry and popped it into his mouth. He lay back in the sand, and more juice trickled from his mouth.

'He scribbles.' Sam was lying beside me with his eyes shut. His warm hand was holding my sandy foot. 'And scrawls, with paint or just a pencil. I don't know what he thinks gives him the right to go to art college.'

'They accepted me. I seem to please them. You're just a barbarian. An Irish barbarian to boot. Bet you wouldn't know the difference between Picasso and Klimt.'

'Who cares about Picasso or whoever? A handful of bourgeois snobs. Elitists.'

'Luckily more than a handful.'

'Tripe. I bet you there's no one within ten miles of here who has ever heard of either of them.'

'Your parents . . .'

'Two bourgeois snobs, penniless to boot, because

they spent all their inherited wealth on sending us off to schools where we would learn useless things about useless people and become bourgeois snobs like themselves. Bloody useless. That's what I think. But it will all change, you'll see.'

I wriggled my foot free from his hand and stood up. 'I'm going to swim. Don't fight. Not on such a lovely day. I'm going to wash the sand off myself and get dressed. We'll have to go home soon.'

They didn't seem to hear me. I walked away from them down over the warm wrinkled sand and into the sea. The tide was coming in, each little wave slapping over the last one, devouring the beach. The water was not cold, the cow still bellowed in the distance and I could hear their young male voices arguing softly behind me. I wondered who Klimt was and I wondered what it must feel like to be seventeen and what bourgeois meant and I dipped my hands in the sea and rubbed my body with my fingers until my hands became gritty with golden grains of sand.

'Bourgeois.' I repeated the word to myself. 'Bourgeois, bourgeois.'

When I came out of the water they were standing on

the sand fully dressed holding my big towel out between them. They wrapped it round me and Sam hoisted me over his shoulder and carried me up to the grass.

'Baby, Baby,' he said as he walked up the beach. 'Marcus and I are best friends. You must remember that. Such enwranglements mean nothing.'

'Polly, Polly, pretty Polly, it's true.' Marcus smiled his nice smile at me as he spoke.

Sam dumped me on the grass beside my clothes. 'Get dressed quickly or we'll be late for dinner.'

Practically the only unpardonable sin at Kildarragh was to be late for dinner. It was rude to Sadie, Grandma would say, and it really annoyed Grandpa. Grandma would storm on Sadie's behalf and Grandpa on his own. 'This is my house,' I heard him shout once at Paddy. 'And I want to eat my dinner at eight o'clock. Not five to eight or five past eight. Eight o'clock. Do you understand?' And Paddy had muttered, 'Yes, sir.' And Pluto had banged his tail against the table leg. Grandpa had turned then to Grandma who was sitting in her chair at the end of the table. 'Am I a domestic tyrant, Beatrice?' 'No, my darling, of course you're not. No one could ever accuse you of that.' There was a ripple of laughter around the table and all was well.

'What's a tyrant, Grandma?'

She was writing letters, sitting at her small desk by the window. Outside was all grey and green and the sky promised rain. I see pictures of those days so clearly in my mind, snapshots tinted with seasonal colour. She put her pen down and looked at me. She always gave her complete attention to whomever she might be addressing.

'A tyrant, my darling, is not a very nice person, and there have been far too many of them in the world. A man of power who rules with an iron rod. Probably a little mad. Yes, mad. I think you could call them that. Hitler was a tyrant, and I am sure that Stalin is one too. They are people who do not know the meaning of the word compassion. Some people believe that Oliver Cromwell was a tyrant, others think he was an enlightened man. He didn't behave well here in Ireland, that's for sure, but we didn't want to be conquered, and he felt he had to conquer us, for God, as well as the Commonwealth, you understand. Your grandfather is not a tyrant, Polly dear, just in case that is what is on your mind. He is a soft and gentle man who shouts from time to time.' She picked up her pen. 'Run along, darling, this is my letter-writing day.'

*   *   *

Then Pluto died.

I would have been about fourteen, full of my own happenings, school, hockey matches, my friends, the cinema on Saturday evenings and long bicycle rides into County Wicklow, to the Cherry Orchard, or the beach at Greystones, where the sea was a bitter challenge which my friends and I found hard to resist.

It had been a day full of wind and little skiffs of rain and we had cycled up to the Featherbed, where we had lit a fire in a tumbledown shed and eaten our sandwiches and chatted and scrambled over the rocks and heather and dipped our feet in bog holes before eating some more sandwiches and cycling home again through the rain. I was wet and smoky and had just taken off my shoes in the hall when Charles put his head round the door.

'God, Polly, you look like a refugee from some civil war or other. Your uncle Sam rang to tell you that Pluto had died.'

'Pluto?' My heart started to thump. 'What did you say about Pluto?'

'He's dead. Gone to the happy hunting ground.'

I must have changed colour because he took a step towards me and put his hand on my shoulder.

'He was old, Polly. You could hardly have expected him to live for ever.'

'Pluto. Nonie. He wasn't old. He was only a little bit older than me. Nonie. I have to go there. I must.'

I began to cry and my mother came rushing down the stairs. She put her arms around me.

'What is the matter, dear one? What is all this hullaballoo about?'

'Pluto. Charles says he's dead.'

'Oh, darling. Charlie, what . . . ?'

'Sam rang. He said to tell Polly. You were out with the kids when he rang.'

'I must go there.'

'Hang on a minute. Let's get this straight. Pluto died. Yes? And you feel a serious need to go to Kildarragh, yes? Get me some Kleenex from the kitchen, Charlie. Come on, you're behaving like a baby. I know you loved Pluto, everyone loved Pluto, but dogs die. You have to get used to death happening. I'm sorry. I'm really sorry. You can't go down there now, in term time, but the moment the holidays start you can go. They'll probably have a new puppy by then and everyone will be happy. Thanks.' She took a bunch of Kleenex from Charles and handed them to me.

'Grandpa needs me.'

'You are not going to Kildarragh. Grandpa will recover without you. I know he'll be sad, darling, but he will recover.'

'He might die too.' The thought of such a thing made me cry even harder.

Nonie sighed. 'Well I think he will recover. Now go and wash your face and you'll feel better. You can write him a letter. That's a good idea.'

'If Greg had still been here he would have gone down there. He would have brought me with him. We would both have gone together.'

She took her hand from my head.

'I think,' she said after a moment, 'that you should go up to your room and gather your thoughts. You've had a nasty shock, but after all a dog is just a dog.'

'Pluto . . .'

'Is just a dog. Was just a dog.'

'Greg . . .'

'On. Up to your room.' She stood up. She sounded cross.

'Maybe Sam will ring me.'

'I wouldn't bet on it. Off you go, there's a good girl, and do your homework. That'll take your mind off Pluto.'

Sam didn't ring; instead he arrived the following afternoon, not long after I had come in from school. I opened the door when the bell rang and was astonished to see him standing there on the step.

'Baby,' he said and opened his arms. We stood on the step and cried, our arms wrapped round each other.

'Baby, Baby.'

'Sam.'

'What's all this row about? Oh, Sam. It's you. Come in.' My mother was standing in the hall looking slightly displeased. Sue was beside her pulling at her skirt.

We moved into the hall, still clutching at each other, still sniffling. In spite of my sniffling I was glad to see him, happy to have his arms wrapped round me.

'My Sam.'

'Who is that man? Why is Polly crying?' Sue pulled again at Nonie's skirt. 'Mummy, Mummy.'

'He is Polly's uncle.'

'And my uncle?'

'No, darling. Polly's uncle.'

'Why is he crying?'

'Why are you both crying? Tell the child, for God's sake. Tell us all.'

'I waited until I knew you'd be back from school,' said Sam. 'I knew I'd bawl and I didn't want to bawl over poor Nonie. Sorry, Nonie. Sorry, little person.'

'I am Sue. Why are you not my uncle?'

'Let's go and sit down,' Nonie suggested, and we followed her into the sitting room.

'Why?'

'I'm just not, but I could pretend to be. How would you like that?'

She suddenly became shy; she hid her face on her mother's lap. 'Brrrm,' she said. 'Brrrm, brrrm.'

'Silly billy.' Nonie ruffled her hair. 'It's lovely to see you, Sam. It's been an age. Will you stay the night?'

'No thanks. I must go back. I stole the father's car; he'll be fit to be tied if he finds out. I just had to catch a sight of Ba— Polly. I had to shed a little tear with her. You may think it's daft, but that's why I came, because the dog is dead and I had to shed a little tear with Polly.'

Nonie looked at him with scorn. 'You're as bad as Polly. Such a to-do about a dog.'

'We loved him for sixteen years. He was older than Polly.'

'Will you have tea or a drink?'

'You are a treasure. Tea, I think, and a spot of bread and jam, then I'll take to the road again.' He took my hand and we followed Nonie into the kitchen.

'Why are you not my uncle? Answer me that.'

'Well, little curiosity-killed-the-cat person, once upon a time . . .'

'I don't want once upon a time, I want a true story.'

'Cross my heart and hope to die this is a true story.'

'Is it, Mummy?'

'Let's hear it and then I'll tell you.' She pulled the kettle over on to the hot plate of the Aga and then proceeded to put cups and saucers on the table.

'Once upon a time there was a beautiful lady called Nonie . . .'

'Mummy.'

'She's always been Nonie to me. Anyway, she met this handsome man called Greg, who came from a big family. There were six of them: Greg, Harry, Jassie, Mickey, Patrick and Sam.'

'You?'

He bowed towards her. 'Me.'

She stood beside him now, one elbow on the kitchen table, staring into his face.

'And Pluto,' I said. 'Don't forget Pluto.'

He smiled. 'And Pluto, of course.'

'Well?'

'Well, Greg and Nonie fell in love and got married and had a little baby called Polly.'

She didn't move her eyes from his face. 'I know Polly.'

'Now the story gets a bit sad. Greg goes off to fight in a war and is killed, so Nonie and Polly are left alone; after a while Charles comes along and makes Nonie happy again and they get married and have Sue and . . .'

'Shane.'

'Yes, Shane, and they all live happily ever after and I am not your uncle, so that's that.'

'But I could pretend.'

'If you really wanted to. I don't see why not. Do you, Baby?' He squeezed my fingers so hard as he spoke that I thought the blood might stop circulating.

'We'll share you.'

Sue stepped away from Sam and did a little twirling dance around the floor. 'Now I have an uncle and Shane doesn't.'

'You'll have to share him with Shane too,' said Nonie. 'It wouldn't be fair if you didn't.'

'No.' Sue screamed the word and then began to cry.

'Hey, hey, easy on. No tears. I don't want a niece who cries and yells. That's baby stuff.'

The little girl beat with her fists on Sam's knees. 'No,' she yelled. 'No share with Shane.'

Nonie took hold of her and gently pushed her towards the door. 'Upstairs, darling. If you're going to scream it must be upstairs. In your room. You can come down when you stop. Go on, off you go.'

'No share with Shane.'

'Upstairs.' Nonie shut the kitchen door and we all listened for a moment to Sue's receding shouts as she slowly climbed the stairs.

'Who'd have children?' sighed Nonie as she poured boiling water into the teapot.

'Who'd be an uncle?' He took my hand in his again and squeezed my fingers.

'How's Grandpa?'

'I don't honestly know. He found Pluto dead on his rug. You know Sadie used to bring up a biscuit for Pluto when she brought up Father's tea in the morning, well he gave a little whistle and Pluto didn't move a muscle, so he picked up the biscuit and went over to see what was up and found that the poor old fellow had died in the night. Died in his sleep. What a way to go, Baby, what a way to go. So he let a roar out of him that you could have heard in Galway city and we all fell out of our beds and went running to his room. He was kneeling on the floor by the poor dead dog and he was roaring "May God be fucked" and Mama was shushing him and Sadie began to cry too. When I came in he got to his feet and said, "Sam, bury that dog," and he left the room and went along the passage and shut himself in the library. Harry came over later in the day and he wouldn't let him in. I haven't seen him since. I ...' He waved his hands distractedly above his head and I thought he was going to cry again, but he didn't. 'The only thing I could think of doing was to come up and see Baby.' He pulled me to him and buried his face in my hair. 'My Baby.'

Nonie sighed. She poured out a cup of tea for him and pushed it across the table.

'I love ya, Baby.'

'You're all cracked,' she said. 'I bet you didn't carry on like this when Greg was killed. Or Jassie. What's happened to your sense of decorum? Didn't you learn about that at school? Eat your bread and jam and think about decorum. Do you want tea, Polly?'

'No thanks.'

'Fuck decorum,' he muttered into my hair.

'I want to go back with Sam. Please may I?'

'Don't be silly, darling. We've had this conversation before. You can go down when you get your holidays. They'll be settled then. This would not be a good time for you to appear. You'd upset them even more. Now, enough tears. Tell me what you're up to, Sam.'

'Nothing much, long vac, just mooching and doing a bit of work for exams. Nothing to write home about.' He gave me a sideways look and I knew he was not telling the truth.

'Pull yourself together, Polly. Enough of this nonsense. I will have to go up and pacify that child, otherwise she'll not stop that noise for hours. There's lots of bread and jam, Sam, if you feel the need.'

She left the room and we were silent until we heard her feet reaching the top of the stairs. He took a handkerchief from his pocket and mopped at his face, wiped his eyes.

'Oh, Baby, it's been so grim. I just had to get out. I had to see your funny old face. I had to hear your voice . . . you see I'm going to make matters worse. I'm going away.'

'Away?'

'Yes. It's a secret, though. I'm not going back to Cambridge next term.'

'Sam . . .'

'There is nothing you can say. I've thought very long and hard about it. They don't know and you must keep your lips buttoned.'

'But where . . .'

'I'm going to Cuba.'

'Cuba? What on earth are you going to Cuba for? What happens in Cuba? Where on earth is it anyway?'

'You'll have to trust me on this. There's no time to tell you the whole story now. I will, though. I promise. It's a whole new experiment in living. I'm going with some pals. We want to be part of it. In on the ground floor, so to speak. We want to see if it works. The Russians have made such a balls of things, but maybe this will work. The Castro brothers—'

'Shut up, Sam. You can't do this to them. You can't just disappear. You must tell Grandpa.'

'They are not to know. You hear me? I promise I will write and tell them everything. You are not to say a word. Not to anyone.'

I shook my head.

'Please, Baby. There are so many people in the world who have no one to speak for them. Oppressed people, almost slaves. I believe I have a duty towards them, to fight for them if need be. They have nothing, men and women with no voices. Oppressed people. Oppressed people.' He whispered the words. 'You will understand when you are grown up.'

'You say you are grown up?'

'Of course.'

'And yet you cry about a dead dog?'

'I thought that you might understand now. That's why I told you. I thought that in two years you might come out there and join me. We could both fight for a new world.'

'I don't care about a new world. I love the old one. Wait just a few years. Finish at Cambridge. Think of Grandma and Grandpa. Please, Sam, can't you wait?'

He took both my hands and pulled me towards him. 'This is my life. They've had theirs. I love them, honestly I do, but they must see that I have the right to do what I want with my own life. You may think I'm a coward, but I am going to go without telling them. I will write to them. I won't just disappear, I promise you that. I will write. I will explain. By post.'

'Coward indeed.'

He let go of my hands. 'Baby!'

'And stop calling me that idiotic name. I hate it.'

I was going to cry again. There were no tears of

sorrow left for poor Pluto, but tears of absolute rage were bubbling up behind my eyes and my head was starting to ache.

'I hate you too. How can you do such a thing to them? They're old. They love you . . . and Sadie too. She loves you. She'll break her back and her heart trying to pick up the pieces if you do this. How can you be so beastly?' I struck out at him. He caught my fist and held it tight. His fingers were strong and fierce; they felt like metal bars pushing their way through my skin. Hurting. 'You're hurting me.'

He let go.

'What are you two fighting about?' Nonie had come back into the room. 'I just get Sue to calm down and then you two start. You're too old for this sort of nonsense, Sam. Polly, wipe your face. You're a sight to behold.'

I was staring at his fingermarks on my arm and I suddenly remembered the day on the haystack. He always won. He always got the last word. It had seemed to me then that he was always right, but this couldn't be right, I thought. Not right to go like this, leave those dear people. I would have to go down and live with them, hold them together. Bloody school, I thought. They would never let me go to the local school. They would never let me stay there. He would be gone and they would slowly fade away out of happiness, out of life. The world would be so dark without them. The house would crumble away; no one would laugh there any more. It would become a disfigurement on the landscape. On stormy nights the slates would blow from the roof, the glass in the windows would crack; weeds would choke the stable yard, brambles ramp over the grey walls, desolation wrap the whole place in its arms. I was in a trance of misery. Their voices fizzed and droned above my head. Nonie put an arm gently round my shoulders.

'You look as though you're in some miserable dream. Wake up. Sam says he's going. He must not be late for dinner.'

Sam held out his hand towards me. 'Bye, Polly. Come down as soon as you can.'

I nodded. 'I'm sorry.' I touched his hand and he grinned at me.

'I'm sorry too. Everything will be OK, though.' He kissed Nonie and then vanished out of the door. I stood on the spot and listened to the hall door close and his feet marching to the gate.

'What's he up to?' Nonie asked. 'No good, I'll be bound.'

'I hope he drives carefully. Grandpa will be raging if his car gets bumped.'

I didn't sleep that night; not a wink. Every time I closed my eyes I saw pictures of the devastated house and heard the crying wind in the ruins, or was that sound the ghosts of the Mahonys longing to be alive again? Why did Sam need to change the world? The question rolled round and round in my head. Was it brave or stupid? I didn't know. I didn't know anything. I must grow up. I must learn. I must look and consider.

I love ya, Baby. The rough whispering voice and the feeling of his fingers in my hair. I shivered. I burrowed under the bedclothes and put my fingers in my ears, but the voice was in my head and nothing could stop the sound of it. At that moment of mournfulness I knew I loved him too in spite of my anger.

I love ya, Baby.

Oh, Sam. I wish I were a grown-up person.

✳   ✳   ✳

Dear Polly (you see, I have remembered) Wolly Doodle,

In spite of that I am a serious fellow. I am just passing through Cambridge, picking up my belongings and also my partner in crime. I HAVE NOT YET TOLD THE PARENTS. But I will, I promise you I will. Before too long. I was just not late for dinner. No time to pee or wash the hands. The old man growled at me when I said that I had been to Dublin and back in his car to see you. But only growled. I told them that you would be down as soon as school was over and they smiled with pleasure, though Mama thinks that you might be lonely here now without anyone of your age. Thanks a lot, I said to her and she sighed. We are all getting so old, she said, too old for a little girl of fourteen, and Father growled again. They do need you, Baby (oops). I will write when I get settled in and tell you my address, so that you can write and tell me all that is happening. I know I will miss you all, you most of all dear Polly Wolly Doodle, but growing up is about teaching yourself to cope with the movements that do take place in all our lives and I do have a dream. I know you may not like my dream, but none the less it is brave and right and must be followed. I do love you, little girl of fourteen, and as you get bigger and older and

seventeen, eighteen, nineteen I will probably love you more
than I do now and perhaps, perhaps, whoa there whoa ...
Bye bye blackbird, blackbird bye bye.

No address, just *Cambridge* written at the top. What
had that place done to him, I wondered.

I read his letter several times that day, inspecting
each word with care. I folded it neatly and put it into
my school satchel, then thought better of that and put
it into the leather writing case with my initials on it that
Nonie had given me for my birthday. I smoothed it out
and tucked it in behind the blue Basildon Bond that
had come with the case. Only a spy, I thought, would
find it there, and there were no spies in our house and
no need for spies.

'Who was that letter from that you got this morning?'
Nonie asked. I was doing my homework, French verbs.

I frowned. 'How,' I asked her, 'would you say if I
were to give it to you would you be pleased?' I felt my
face getting red. 'In French.'

'Um. Subjunctive? Conditional?'

'Something dopey like that.'

'You must work it out for yourself. Who?'

'Who what?'

'Was the letter from?'

'If I were to tell you would you be pleased? Sam.'

'I presume he got safely home. How are his parents?'

'OK.'

'Did he get into trouble?'

'He didn't say. *Si je t'aurais le donne …*'

Nonie sighed. 'French has never been one of my strong points. Why was he writing?'

I thought for a moment or two. '*Pourquoi il m'a écrit? Je ne sais pas, Maman. Peut-être il était* lonely.'

'*Peut-être.*' Nonie left the room.

❋   ❋   ❋

'What is love?' I don't know when I asked Grandma that question, or indeed why. Had I been reading something that had disturbed my mind or had I been thinking about the defection of Sam; I really don't know. We must have been in her sewing room, a small room halfway up the stairs into which the sun poured in the mornings; in the afternoons it became grey and almost unfriendly. Here she would sit surrounded by shirts missing buttons, socks to be darned and sheets that needed patching. She had a long box with compartments in which she kept needles and thread, buttons, and a collection of little thimbles, some of real silver, to fit fingers of all sizes. There were safety pins and ordinary pins, hooks and eyes, rolls of elastic, wool for the darning and a wooden mushroom for pushing into the sock so that you could darn with care and make no lumps.

She put her sewing carefully down on the table, took off her glasses and pinched the top of her nose with her fingers.

'That, dear Polly, is a very complicated question. There are so many answers. Yes.' She stared out of the window, screwing up her eyes against the sun, searching for words, for where to begin to answer my complicated question. Of course it didn't seem like a complicated question to me and I sat waiting for her to answer me.

'Your grandpa and I love each other, but that is a story in itself. A story of ups and downs, of fighting, of passion, of fun and terrific sadness, of *enduring*. Perhaps that is what love is, enduring. I don't mean to sound gloomy, chicken, but that element of love has to be faced. When you're young and dizzy, you believe in getting married and living happily ever after, in princes and princesses . . . well, for heaven's sake, look what happens to princes and princesses nowadays. Treachery, loneliness, sorrow, war, death . . . all those things happen to us all and some of us are lucky enough to be sustained through them by love. Maybe I'm talking rubbish but you didn't give me much time to think.'

She squeezed her eyes tight shut and sat in silence, and I sat and looked at her old wrinkled face and wondered what the world would be like without her. Her voice when she spoke was a whisper and I had to lean towards her to catch the words as they fell from her mouth.

' "Beareth all things, believeth all things, hopeth all things, endureth all things . . . And now abideth faith, hope, charity, these three; but the greatest of these is charity." St Paul wrote that. A bit of a bastard I've always thought, but wise in spots. Yes. Anyway, I think love is the word he meant here, not charity. That's just my view. Sex is, of course, something else, very troublesome at times, wonderful at others. You might say that sex is very seductive.' She laughed a quiet laugh at her own joke. 'I suppose that the true love is the love that parents have for their children. Unequivocal, universal. I would think that if one of your children turned out to be an axe murderer, you'd still love him. Maybe not. Maybe not. It seems like an easy word to talk about, but it's not, dear Polly. I suppose that everyone has their own personal views, even whimsical notions. It doesn't do to be too whimsical about love, though. You must remember its size. It is very big; huge, in fact . . .' She put her hands up to her face and began to cry. I stood up and took a step towards her, then stopped. I didn't know what to say.

'Don't cry, Grandma. I'm sorry. I'm sorry. I'm sorry.'

What was I sorry for? I didn't know, but I felt it was my fault, this waterfall of tears. She took a handkerchief from her pocket and wiped her eyes; she blew her nose, she smiled at me.

'What a silly old woman I am,' she said.

* * *

Sam wasn't true to his word: he didn't write to his parents; he didn't write to me. I only realised this when I went down to Kildarragh after the school holidays had started. Only six weeks had passed since he had called on us and I hadn't expected any sound from him, but I had hoped that he would have written to them and explained his disappearance. They didn't seem to realise that he had disappeared; not even Harry knew anything about his movements.

'Sam? God no, never hear from him. He's not the world's greatest communicator,' was his comment when I asked him whether he had had any news from his brother. 'Why do you ask?'

'No reason. It's just strange him not being here in the summer.'

'Maybe he's working for a change. Or maybe he has a lovely girl over there. Who can tell?'

Harry didn't care. All his energies that summer were going into his courtship of Katie Whelan, the doctor's daughter, who had suddenly burst upon the world as a charming girl with a huge boisterous laugh and freckles all over her nose. She was only five years older than I was, the same age in fact as Sam, and my grandparents couldn't make their minds up as to whether she was the right girl for Harry or not.

'Better than a city girl.'

'Her father's a decent chap.'

'She's too young for him.'

'*Ne temere.*' Grandpa growled the words. I didn't know what they meant, but he made them sound menacing.

I didn't say a word; I looked at Grandma's face, and she smiled thinly at me.

'Silly talk,' she said. End of conversation.

* * *

The thunderstorm happened the night before I was due to go home. The day had been menacing, promising unpleasantness: solid grey clouds were shifted by a warm breeze, which barely moved the branches of the trees; the long grass didn't stir and there was no sound from the sea, which lay grey and oily reflecting the sky, neither waves nor fish nor birds disturbing its surface. Neither flicks nor flashes. We even found it hard to move; the atmosphere weighed us down, anchored us to the ground. Grandma dozed in her winter garden, a book on her knee, while Grandpa strode up and down in his room, backwards and forwards, from time to time banging his stick on the floor in some sort of frenzy of rage. Sadie was stirring

a huge pot in the kitchen when I brought the goose-
berries in to her.

'That's the girl. There's a bowl on the table if you'd
top and tail them for me. The girls are doing the
bedrooms today and taking their time about it.
Would you have tea or elderflower? Sit up to the table
there now and take the weight from your feet. It's a
horrible day. A real day for dead men; they might
enjoy it, but surely no one else will. We'll have a storm
tonight, sure as eggs is eggs, and the mistress will
have us all in the dining room with the curtains pulled
tight. What will it be?'

I chose elderflower.

She was right: about eleven o'clock that night, just
after I had gone to bed, the black sky was torn apart by
the most ferocious flash of lightning that I have ever
seen and then almost in the same breath came a crash of
thunder that rolled and rattled around in the darkness.
It sounded to me as though a war was going on, being
fought over us and around us, almost it seemed in the
middle of the house. This bastion of ours became very
vulnerable. I lay shaking in my bed, my head under the
pillows, until I heard Grandma's voice calling, 'The

dining room. Quick. Everyone. Downstairs. Before the next crash. Quick. Now.'

Outside in the darkness I could hear the horses kicking the wooden walls of their boxes.

'Down, down, now. Don't turn the lights on. Now.'

The last word had become a little squawk. There was a crack and the next sheet of lightning lit the world. I threw myself out of bed and ran to the door; the landing was dark and over the banisters I could see a glimmer of light coming from the dining room. As I made my way down the stairs towards the glimmering light the thunder rolled again. It must be like a war, I thought, and then I heard a deep voice behind me.

'*Dies irae, dies illa, solvet saeclum in favilla . . .*'

Grandpa was on the stairs behind me, his voice declamatory.

'. . . *teste David cum Sibylla*. Who's that? Oh, ah, Miss Polly. *Dies irae . . .*'

The thunder stopped and in the darkness his voice echoed round the hall. Grandma came to the dining room door, candle in hand, and peered through the dark at the pair of us.

'. . . *dies illa . . .*'

'What in the name of God are you shouting about? Come, precious Polly. We have candles in here and tea. We will have tea, won't we, Sadie?'

'If the Lord lets us live we'll have tea.'

'The Lord seems to be pretty angry with us at the moment. I felt Latin was the only language in which to address the situation. I don't remember a storm in all my life as noisy as this one, as dramatic I should really say . . . a Götterdämmerung storm. What do you think, my darling?'

'Sit down and don't be foolish.'

'Why, anyway, may we not stay in our beds?' He sounded aggrieved.

'Sit down, for heaven's sake. You know as well as I do how dangerous these storms can be. Remember when the roof was ripped off the Bank of Ireland and the Morrisons' chimney stack was hit? Paddy Feeny was killed . . .'

'Silly bugger was sheltering under a tree. We all know—'

'The meat-packing factory in Gort went up in flames and—'

One of the girls started to cry as a rip of lightning

came through the heavy curtains. For a second their startled faces were floodlit and they looked like characters in some old horror movie. Sadie got to her feet.

'I'll make tea.' She started for the door.

'Sadie, sit down. I—'

'Tea. That's what we all need, and if the kitchen is hit by one of them bolts, then give me a good funeral. But I don't think that God needs me yet. Come along now, girl dear, and give me a hand with the cups.' She beckoned to the girl who wasn't crying. 'And you, stop your sniffling or I'll send you home to your mammy first thing in the morning.' She opened the door and they went out into the dark hall to a drum roll of thunder.

'Personally,' said Grandpa, 'I'd rather have a large Scotch and soda.'

Grandma laughed. 'Sit down and shut up,' she said.

So we sat round the long table and our faces flickered in the light from the candles and the only sound was the quiet sobbing from the girl. Grandma took a handkerchief from the pocket of her dressing gown and passed it along the table to her.

'Wipe your nose, child, and dry your eyes. Everything's going to be all right.'

'We used to sit in here during the Civil War,' said Grandpa suddenly. 'Just like this, candles and all, we hadn't any electricity in those days, waiting for them to come and burn the house down. We didn't know who it would be, but we just knew they would come. This room was our little fortress. Only, of course, you must understand, when there was trouble in the district. Otherwise we didn't do such foolish things as sit up all night waiting to be burnt out. We just went about our business. Farming was our business. Still is. Yes. Harry's business now, thank God. All I can do nowadays is read. Don't have to worry about someone coming to set the place on fire. I like reading. Thank God for the electricity. Now, Beatrice, if you weren't a domestic tyrant you would allow us to have the lights on and we could all read. We could pass the time most usefully. Polly reads, don't you, Polly? I have seen you escaping from the library with books tucked under your arm. Mighty tomes. I always hope that you will bring them back and replace them correctly.'

'I do, Grandpa, I promise you.'

'That's my girl.'

He got up and went over to the sideboard and helped himself to some whisky and then added some soda water from the siphon that was standing there.

'Beatrice?'

'No thanks. I'll wait for Sadie's tea.'

He stood peering through the golden light at each one of us in turn, then slowly made his way to the chair he always sat in to eat his meals, the high carver at the end of the table. He took a long slow drink and then sat down.

'Tell me, Polly.' He leant towards me as he spoke. 'Where is Sam?'

I felt my face getting red. I knew that they couldn't see it in the candlelight. I squirmed. The thunder rattled, quite far away; the girl had stopped crying as if she too wanted to hear the answer to the question.

'Isn't he in Cambridge?'

Silence.

'How should I know? Haven't you heard from him?'

'We thought, your grandmother and I, that he might have told you what his plans were.' His voice was gentle.

'Why would he tell me?'

'He might have written to you.'

I shook my head. Damn Sam, I thought in my head, damn, damn.

'We do worry, you know. We get anxious. You know nothing of some madcap plan?'

'Marcus might know.'

'Marcus might not tell us. They are pals, you know. Pals sometimes don't speak secrets.'

I nodded. I blushed even more. The thunder growled. The door opened and Sadie came into the room carrying the teapot, followed by the girl with a tray which she put on the table.

'And some cocoa I made for Baby. Hot, strong tea is not the thing for a young stomach. Drink that up now, little pet, and we'll all be back in our beds in a twinkling.'

She passed me a mug of cocoa. Diminished lightning flashed for moment through the curtain and the steam from the cocoa rose warm into my face.

'Sadie, what would we do without you?' Grandma sighed. Sadie laughed and poured tea. The thunder rattled, but more quietly now than it had done before.

Grandpa put his empty glass down on the table.

'I'll have tea too, and some of that cake. It looks good. It reminds me . . .' He stopped and I knew he was remembering the cake she had wrapped up and given to Harry when he was off to the war, made with Guinness and some of his own port.

I wondered what had happened to that cake; had my father ever got to eat a piece of it, or had Harry shared it with his new friends at some training camp in England? Or had he, bored with carrying its weight around, thrown it into the sea from the Mail Boat?

I sipped at my cocoa and Sadie cut great slices of cake, much larger than daytime slices I thought as I watched her.

Grandma picked up her cup of tea and folded her two hands round its warmth. Slowly she walked round the table and sat down by me. She placed the cup on the table and touched my arm.

'If you knew anything, would you tell us? If you find anything out, would you tell us? If you get a letter from him, would you . . . ? Would you, Polly, would you?'

I shook my head. I wanted to cry. 'I don't know. Grandma, I honestly don't know.'

'You see, we worry. You must know that. We've lost two of our lovely people already, and I know we've got you instead and that is very special, but still we don't want to lose another one. Grandpa's heart would break.'

Sadie turned her attention from the cake-cutting and pointed the knife at Grandma. 'Isn't she only young yet? Don't try to bully her into telling you things she knows nothing about. Sam'll let you know in his own good time what he's up to. He's a good lad. Cake, Baby?'

I took a huge piece. 'Thanks.'

My grandmother stroked my arm for a moment and then there was an almighty crash of thunder and the lightning sliced in through the curtains again and one of the girls screamed.

'What did I say to you about the roaring and screaming? I'll send you home to your mammy tomorrow so I will.'

'Sorry, Sadie. I just got a fright. I won't do it again.' She wiped her face and hiccuped. The thunder rolled away once more and rain could be heard beating down on roofs and windows.

'There now,' said Grandpa. 'It will all be over soon. Three hearty cheers. We'll all be tucked up in our warm beds and sleep will come. We will forget your grandmother's thundery nightmare. "Sleep that knits up the ravelled sleeve of care, The death of each day's life, sore labour's bath, Balm of hurt minds, great nature's second course, Chief nourisher in life's feast."'

'That is the Scottish play. You must not quote the Scottish play. You know that as well as I do.' Grandma sounded aggrieved.

'Why not?' I asked.

'"Glamis hath murdered sleep, and therefore—"'

'Do stop, my darling. This moment. Bad luck, Poll. It's very bad luck to quote *Macbeth*.'

'Myths, legends, superstitious nonsense. Pay no heed.' Grandpa waved his arms in the air, rather like a windmill, I thought. I had never seen a windmill, but the notion sprang into my mind as I watched his arms flailing. The door opened and Harry came running in, water dripping from him with every movement, bringing with him the sound of rolling thunder.

'God! What rain. I'm drownded.' He shook himself like a dog coming out of the sea. 'I thought you'd be up, marshalled by Mama into the dining room. Whoopee. I was right and so I'm drownded. Just that quick run from the car to the hall door. Swoosh. I thought I should come and tell you: I'm engaged. Katie said yes. This very evening. Everything by the book, Mama. I've spoken to her father. He is so pleased, and her mother . . . I left them opening a bottle of champagne and rushed home to tell you. Isn't it splendid? Don't you think it's splendid, Sadie?'

'A wedding! Won't that be great? The last wedding here was Polly's father and that was just as that awful war was starting and anyway they got married in Dublin and never said a word about it to us until it was signed and sealed.' She threw her arms around him and hugged him tight.

Grandma got to her feet, a bright smile on her face. 'Darling, that is wonderful. I'm so happy. They must all come and have dinner tomorrow night. We'll celebrate then. What a shame Polly will have gone.' She took Harry's face between her two hands and gazed lovingly into his eyes. 'So happy, my darling boy.'

Grandpa had retreated to the sideboard where he was busy pouring himself some more whisky. His hand was shaking as he poured. Words tumbled from his lips like the whisky tumbling from the decanter into the glass.

'Why do we have children?'

'Darling!'

'Why? Why? What do they bring us? Hey?'

'Sadie, take the girls and go to bed. The storm is over. Turn on the lights as you leave the room. Let's cast some light . . .'

'They bring you tears and tears. And the bloody dog is dead too.'

'Darling, Harry isn't dead, he's here. In this room. He's just got engaged. An occasion of happiness. Future generations and all that.'

'It's not just death that brings you tears . . .'

Sadie hustled the girls out of the room. They looked as if they would rather stay.

'Father . . . I thought you liked Katie.'

'Katie is a charming girl. I have absolutely nothing against Katie.' He threw some whisky down his throat. 'For hundreds of years, father and son, father and son, we have lived here. We have resisted successfully the bondage of Rome. We haven't kicked up a fuss; we haven't barred our doors to anyone, we have been liberal and thoughtful in our dealings with everyone. Everyone. And now I am promised that my grandchildren will be imprisoned behind the bars of that illiberal church. Is it any wonder that I cry?'

'Father! No one has mentioned children. I am getting married—'

'And the natural outcome of marriage? Don't tell me that you are planning to have a childless union?'

'Geoffrey!' Grandma was getting angry. She hardly ever called him by his name unless she was angry. She marched across the room and took the glass from his hand. 'Come and sit. Let us have no more of this nonsense. You have upset Harry. You are upsetting me.'

'I am not a domestic tyrant.'

'I never said you were. Now stop being foolish and sit down and let's talk calmly.'

There was a long silence and then all three of them took their seats at the table. I didn't dare to move in case I was, like Sadie and the girls, sent to bed.

'You know as well—'

'Father—'

'Now listen here, you two—'

They all spoke at once; then they all stopped and the silence was long and dangerous. Finally Grandpa turned towards Harry.

'*Ne temere.*'

'I never realised you were a bigot, Father.'

'I am not a bigot. No one in my whole life has ever called me a bigot. I will not have such a tag attached to me. Not ever. Nor will I have, as I go to my grave, the knowledge that this house will succumb to Rome. No. Rather than that I will leave the place to Baby. Yes. That's what I will do. Rather than have my dead heart broken the way you are breaking my live one, I will do that thing. If Greg hadn't been killed it would probably have come to her anyway.'

I longed for invisibility, to be able to disappear; I didn't want to listen any more. I didn't want them to remember suddenly that I was there, alarmed by what I was hearing, frightened by Grandpa's anger.

'Geoffrey, you must stop this ridiculous storming. Your imagination is running away with you. The Whelans are reasonable, decent people—'

'I haven't said that they are not. I like them. I like the girl, but—'

'No buts, my darling.'

'Of course there are buts. I don't want my family to be anything but free; free in their actions, in their thinking, in their whole being; responsible freedom. If I prayed I would pray for that.'

'Father ...'

I must have moved because Grandma suddenly became aware of my presence. She came over and put her hand gently on my shoulder.

'Bed, dear child. Go to bed.'

I didn't speak, just nodded and slipped from my chair and left the room, so I didn't hear the rest of their conversation. I lay unhappily in my bed and thought about what the old man had said, and then I thought about Sam, and wondered where he would stand in such a situation.

✳   ✳   ✳

I went home the next morning; one of the men drove me to Galway city and I got the midday train. 'Everything will be all right,' Grandma said to me at the hall door and kissed me and held me tight. She smelled of lavender, I remember. 'We all love you, Polly. Come back as soon as you can. And don't worry; don't be sad, dear girl. Youth's the season made for joy.' She gave me a little push down the steps towards the car. I got in and waved and she waved and Sadie waved from the bottom of the steps and there was no Grandpa and no Harry and my heart trembled inside me. Growing up seemed to be an onerous task. I hoped I would be up to it.

Nonie was at the station waiting for me, no babies, no Charles, no one, just the two of us in the car on the way back to Sandymount.

'Harry's going to be married.'

Nonie didn't speak; she was negotiating the traffic in College Green. She had to concentrate very hard while negotiating traffic.

'Sorry,' she said, when the trouble was over. 'What did you say about Harry?'

'He's getting married.'

'Splendid. Lovely. Who to? Someone nice, I hope. Do you like her?'

'She's OK. She's only five years older than me. Think

of that, Nonie. Five years! She's the same age as Sam. Isn't that extraordinary, in five years I could be getting married.'

'I do hope not.' She manoeuvred her way across the traffic and turned to the right. Someone blew a horn.

'Oh, do shut up,' she shouted out of the window. 'Yes, darling, do go on. Tell me more about the fiancée. Her name, for instance.'

'Katie. Katie Whelan. She's Dr Whelan's daughter.'

'Neat,' said my mother. 'To inveigle a doctor into your family. Are they pleased . . . your grandparents?'

'We-ell . . . Grandpa had a fit when Harry told us. He shouted and roared.'

'Good heavens!'

'I don't know what happened then. Grandma sent me to bed. I think everything will be all right. She says everything will be all right.'

'How foolish of your grandfather to behave like that. To shout and roar.'

'There was a thunderstorm.'

There was a long silence between us. What a silly thing to say, I thought.

'A thunderstorm?' she said at last.

'Yes. It was on top of the house. Right on top, and Harry came in just as it was calming down a little. Grandma had us all in the dining room.'

My mother laughed. 'She would. I can just see it.'

'He was full of joy and excitement and then Grandpa started shouting at him and it was like the thunder coming into the house and crashing around a bit.'

'But why? He must have had some reason. Did he not like the girl? Her parents? What was his objection?'

'He said he didn't want to have Catholic grand-children.'

She drove into the kerb and put her foot on the brake. We bumped to a standstill; another car blew its horn at us.

'He said what?'

I shook my head at her, feeling foolish; perhaps, I thought, I should have kept my mouth buttoned.

'He seemed to think it wouldn't be a good thing,' I mumbled.

She laughed again, a sort of grim little laugh.

'He doesn't live in the real world. Dear old man. He

can't stop it happening, not if he shouts till the end of time. As if it mattered. As if it bloody mattered.'

'It matters to him.'

'Well it shouldn't.'

She started up again and we drove the rest of the way home in silence.

She didn't talk to me about it again, not a word, but she must have told Charles about our conversation, because a few days later when I was eating my breakfast, hurrying through it as usual, not wanting to be late for school, he came into the dining room and kissed the top of my head.

'Morning, Polly.'

'Morning.'

'Nonie tells me that your uncle Harry is getting married.'

I scooped the remains of my corn flakes into my mouth, picked up my toast and stood up. 'Mmm.'

'I presume that you're going to be a bridesmaid?'

'I shouldn't think so. I must fly. I don't want to be—'

'I gather your grandfather is a bit upset.'

I didn't want to talk to him about it. This was my

family, not really any longer even Nonie's family. My private family: nothing, nothing to do with him. I ran towards the door.

'Can't stay. See you. Bye, Nonie. Bye brats,' I called as I ran down the hall and slammed the door behind me.

They, the brats, always used to stand by the landing window and I would turn at the gate and wave to them and they would wave back; they were sweet kids really. I loved them. That morning I didn't look back up towards them. I slammed the gate and got on to my bike and pedalled off without as much as a peek in their direction. That was the beginning of a whole new year of school, of growing, of trying to understand why grown-ups behaved in the way they did, not very successfully, I'm afraid. Mind you, as I sit here, fifty years on, I have to say that I still don't understand the workings of men's minds. Anyway the strange thing was that three weeks later I received letters from both Grandma and Sam, on the same rainy day. I arrived home from school soaking wet and exhausted having fought the wind and the rain all the way from Morehampton Road to Sandymount, pedalling head down straight into a huge bluster of a north wind, full of rain and muddy water from the puddles on the road. The waves were breaking over the sea road when I got home, licking up the little path between our gate and the hall door. Sue's and Shane's faces were pressed against the drawing room window and behind them I could see Nonie clapping her hands as I came in the gate. When I opened the front door they were all standing in the hall.

'Hurray, she's home. We thought you might be drownded,' said Sue.

'Drownded,' repeated Shane.

'Run up, darling, and have a nice big hot bath.'

'Bath,' repeated Shane.

'I have never seen anyone as wet in my whole life. Have it in my bath and pour in lovely things. You must be frozen.'

'Flozer.'

'Silly Shane. F-r-ozen.'

'Flozer.' He clapped his hands. How wonderful it was to be able to say such a difficult word. 'Polly flozer.'

I threw my coat on to the floor and bent to kiss the

little boy, my frozen cheek resting for a moment against his warm one.

'Clever Shane. Polly is flozer. Polly is going up to jump into Nonie's bath and when she comes down she won't be flozer any more.'

I toed off my shoes and kicked them across the hall and then I saw the two letters on the table. I recognised Grandma's writing, in deepest black ink and written with a fountain pen, no ballpoint for her, big letters striding across the envelope, and she called me Miss; no one else ever wrote that word on an envelope addressed to me. I picked them up and pushed them deep into the pocket of my blazer.

'Is that your grandmother's writing I see?' asked Nonie as I started up the stairs.

'Yes.' My feet began scurrying.

'Who is the other one from?'

'I'm flozer.' I ran on up the stairs and into my bedroom. I took the envelopes out of my pocket and examined the second one. It had come from England; I did not recognise the writing. I was cold, my hands shaking, my shoulders damp with the rain. I could hear Nonie and the children in the room below, Shane shouting 'Flozer' at the top of his voice. I put the unopened envelopes under my pillow and took my towel and dressing gown across the landing to Nonie's bathroom.

I lay unmoving for a long time in the steaming bath; the rain beat relentlessly against the window panes and the warmth seeped back into my body. I drifted into almost sleep, forgetting the letters, lulled by the children's voices and the distant sound of a radio playing.

'Polly. Polly Wolly Doodle. Wake up.'

Nonie's voice calling. I had slept, slipped into sleep. I sat up and felt that the water had cooled a bit, was no longer the comfort wrapper it had been.

'Polly.'

'Yes, coming.' I groped for my towel and got out of the bath. 'I fell asleep. I'm coming.'

The brats were sitting at the kitchen table when I went down, poking bits of toast into boiled eggs. Nonie was smoking as she sat and watched them. The smoke drifted up from her mouth in a corkscrew spiral into the darkness of the high ceiling.

'So?' Nonie smiled at me. 'How is Beatrice?'

'Oh, lordie! I forgot the letter. I went asleep in the bath.'

'Sit down and have your tea now. You can get it later. Charles and I are going out at half past seven, so you'll be in charge.'

'Will you read me a story? A really long story.'

'If you're good I'll read you a short story.'

'A long one.'

'Long one,' Shane repeated, and threw a piece of toast at his sister.

'Hey, hey, baby boy, none of that or there'll be no stories for anyone.' Nonie stubbed out the remains of her cigarette and went round to sit beside her son. So tea went on.

When I got back to my room I took the letters out from under my pillow and opened Grandma's letter.

My darling Polly,

I meant to write to you before, but time has been scarce and also I was not quite sure what to say about that thunderous evening just before you went back home. I hope that you weren't too upset by our strange adult behaviour. Harry went off in a huff and we haven't seen him since

and Grandpa has retreated more or less to the loneliness
of his library where Sadie brings him his meals on a tray. I
tell her that this is silly of her, but she doesn't listen to me.
I went down to the village in the pony and trap and visited
Dr and Mrs Whelan. I haven't told your grandfather that
I have done this yet. I have invited them to dinner in about
three weeks' time and I will summon Mickey and Patrick
from Dublin to come and support me and show family
solidarity. I will keep my fingers and thumbs crossed that
Grandpa will have seen reason by then. I'm sure he will have.
He is not a domestic tyrant. You and I know that, in fact we
all know that. He is old and intemperate but a good and
caring man. If he knew that I was writing to you he would
send kisses. I send them, dear Polly, on his behalf, and of
course also on mine. Be good, work hard and don't let the
nonsensical behaviour of your elders worry you too much or
for too long.

Your loving Grandma.

How I longed at that moment to be down there with her. Grandpa would let me creep into his library and read, curled up in one of the huge chairs. Maybe we wouldn't speak, but he would not be alone. He would hear me breathing, turning the pages, and I would hear him doing the same.

I pushed the letter back into its envelope and laid it on the table beside my bed. I felt anxious; when I picked up the second letter, my hands trembled and the trembling ran up my arms to the back of my neck. I tried to concentrate on the envelope, on the unfamiliar writing. It had to be from Sam. Had to, had to be. I tore the flap open. Inside were several folded bits of paper. The first one that I took out and opened up was a drawing of a small sandy cove with the trees forming a semicircle at the top of a gentle hill sloping down to the sea. I cried out; I couldn't help it. I put it on the bed beside me and stretched it as best I could, smoothed it with my two hands, tried to iron out the creases. There was no gold, only shades of grey, but the magic was there, of that lovely day that we had spent by the sea. Shades of grey, deep dents where the paper had been folded and then wedged into the envelope. I carried it carefully to my writing table where I smoothed it as flat as I could and laid small piles of books on top of it: that was all I could do, that and hope that in the fullness of time the folds would iron out. Of course they haven't; I have it, here on the wall above my desk, neatly framed and glassed, a charming and rather crumpled-looking memory.

Next I unfolded the smaller of the two notes. It was from Marcus. His scrawl was almost illegible, black and spidery, the Scottish name of his parents' house or castle engraved at the top of the page.

Dearest Polly,

I do hope you remember me, if not maybe the enclosed sketch may ring a bell in your head. Your uncle is being elusive and mysterious. I haven't seen him for several months, but a letter arrived the other day from him, via a mutual friend, in which he asked me to post this note on to you. I don't know what the hell he is up to, no good, I'll be bound. But all I can say is that when I last did see him he was not being forthcoming about his future plans and I did not press him on the subject. I am at the moment preparing to go to Paris, where I have wangled my way into the studio of a painter who I hope will prod and push me along the great paths followed by Cézanne, Matisse and of course the golden Klimt. I hope dear Polly that one day our paths may cross again.

And then the flamboyant scrawl of his signature.

Darlingest Baby,

You must be so angry with me. I haven't kept my promise to you. I grovel, I really do. I would be grateful however if you did not tell the aged dears about this letter. Keep mum, please. I don't want them to worry about me. I don't want them to put all sorts of searches in motion, which they might well do. To all intents and purposes I am in Cambridge, being undutiful, but safe, neglecting them shockingly, but safe, Baby. It is most important that they think I am at least safe. You are the only person who knows that I am at loose in the large and dangerous world. Where? you may well ask, but I am not at liberty to tell you. I am not in Cuba yet, and before I do go there I promise that I will come back very briefly to see you and the dears. Do not worry about me, my little darling, just grow bigger and more beautiful so that my heart will break when next I have to leave you. It almost did last time. It is just held together with Sellotape and a bit of string at the moment! Don't pester Marcus, he knows nothing. He was just a convenient postbox.

All my love, S.

Why was I crying?

Sitting on my bed, silently crying. Outside the window, across the road and the two walls, across the wrinkled sand and the great weight of sea, the hill of Howth was beginning to light up. I longed not to be there. I wanted to be in Kildarragh with the aged dears and Sam and Sadie, my people, except of course now I had a secret that would divide me from them. I did not want that secret. I only wanted things to be the way they had been. I didn't like the feeling of growing up. I heard Nonie's voice calling me. I wiped my face with my sleeve; I shoved the letters under my pillow.

'Coming.'

She was standing at the bottom of the stairs looking beautiful, ready to go out with Charles.

'We're off, darling. Are you all right? You're very pink-looking. They're both asleep. They had a great gallop along the beach this afternoon. It really wore them out. We'll be back about elevenish. How's Beatrice?' She was putting on her coat as she spoke.

'Fine.'

'Grandpa?'

'A bit cranky, but fine too.'

'Good, good. Bye, darling. Kiss kiss.'

She was gone out into the dark blue evening to Charles waiting in the car and I returned to my bedroom and my melancholy thoughts.

✳   ✳   ✳

Half term was in October; smells of burning leaves and the sea constantly beating on the shore, rolling and unrolling, grey, blue, green, black, washing disreputable objects up against the sea wall: bicycles, dead dogs, rubber boots, tin cans, scraps of newspapers, all there after each high tide waiting for the council man with the barrow to come and pick them up. Sometimes he wouldn't come for weeks, hoping no doubt that the next high tide would wash them out to sea again. Foghorns from round the bay sounding like wailing, moaning ghosts, singing to the drowned and making you feel happy to be tucked up warm in your bed.

I had gone on and on at Nonie until she had telephoned to Grandma to ask if I could go down to Kildarragh for a few days. I heard her from my bedroom speaking on the telephone. Her voice was low, almost a whisper.

'But,' she said, 'what about Geoffrey? It might be too much for him. Might it not?' She said the last three words with a certain venom and I wondered for the first time if she had had problems in the past with the dear old things. I put my head round the door and tried to hear what Grandma might be saying, but there was only silence.

'You're very kind,' said my mother at last. 'She'll be so pleased. From time to time she pines for you all. You know that teenage stuff they go on with. Long faces, blah blah. How is Sam, by the way? We don't seem to have heard from him for ages.'

I crept out on to the landing, but I still couldn't hear Grandma's voice.

'It's the way of the world, darling. He'll turn up sometime. So, I'll put Polly on the Galway train on Friday. Kiss kiss.' She put down the phone, and I slipped back into my room. I felt like dancing. Tuesday, Wednesday, Thursday and then Kildarragh.

Harry met me at Galway station in his car. It was cold and raining and the town looked grey and uncared for. He had a rug in the back of the car which he tucked round my legs. He was only a year and a half younger than my father would have been. He was losing hair on the top of his head.

'You're going bald,' I said. I patted the balding patch.

'Oh, do shut up, Baby. That's such a pestilential thing to say, especially to someone who has come such a long way to get you. And, what's more, pinched Mother's rug to keep your little legs warm.' He grinned up at me, gave a final tuck and stood up. 'They're so pleased you're coming, Baby. You've no idea. No idea at all.' He stood up and slammed the door of the car and walked slowly round to his own side. He got in and fiddled with the key. 'You've got very pretty and almost grown-up-looking. I think I'll have to call you Polly from now on.' He put the key into the ignition and we were off. It was raining, grey fine rain, and the city was grey and the sky and the glimpses that we caught of the sea, an unfriendly colour, and the wind was blowing off the sea and the smell of salt brushed over us. I was glad that he had brought the rug to keep me warm.

'How are they?' I asked after a while.

'Do you have the faintest idea where Sam is?' His

voice was a mixture of curiosity and anger. 'If you do, Polly, please tell me. It's important. They haven't heard from him. Not a squeak, and it's really debilitating them. You can see. Day by day. The bloody little bastard.' He banged his right hand on the steering wheel. 'Bloody little bastard.'

'Why should I know anything? Why should he let me know anything?'

He put out a hand and touched my shoulder. 'Sorry, old thing. Truly. It's just I'm a bit depressed, that's all.'

'How's Katie? Is that all right?'

'She finds it a bit depressing too. Her mother and father came to dinner last week. The boys came down from Dublin, Sadie pulled out all the stops, Mother looked wonderful and the old man behaved perfectly. He lashed alcohol into us all and everything went perfectly. Well, perfectly-ish.'

'What do you mean by that?'

He reached forward and opened the glove locker, took out a small parcel wrapped in greaseproof paper and handed it to me. 'Sadie said to give you that. She said you might be hungry.'

'Thanks. Yes. Thanks.' I opened the parcel and found two slices of Sadie's brown bread, thickly spread with yellow butter and loganberry jam. 'Oh, Sadie, what would we do without you?'

He laughed, and I took a huge bite. I munched. 'There is a God.' He laughed again. We drove for a little while and I continued to munch, finally wiping my fingers with my handkerchief.

'Well, go on, about Grandpa. What did he say?'

'It was just as we were all leaving, at the hall door. Mama had just kissed Mrs Whelan; we all seemed so happy, everything working right. Father took Dr Whelan by the shoulder, quite firmly, and said, "Just one thing, my dear friend. We all love your daughter but no one, no one, is going to make my son promise away his children's future. So think about that, my friend."'

'Golly,' I said, startled.

'"No swearing, no signing bits of paper, no bloody cabals. I'm warning you, just in case." He was shouting. Mama screeched like a wild old bird and pushed him back in through the door and then slammed it and we were all left outside. Somewhat stunned, I must say.'

'What did Dr Whelan say?'

'He just took Mrs Whelan by the arm and said, "It's the drink talking." She started to cry in the car. Sniffle, snuffle she went all the way home; didn't say a word, just snuffled. When we got to their house he hustled the pair of them out of the car and in through the hall door, then he put his head in the car window and said, "Well, Harry, what did you think of your father's little outburst?" Well, as you can imagine, I didn't know what to say. "It'll sort itself out" was all I could manage. "He's old. He takes little turns like this." "Hmm," says the doctor. "We'll have to have a serious talk, you and I. You are the person of importance, not your father. Personally I don't mind much one way or the other, but it's the women." He put his hand on my shoulder for a moment and then was gone.' He was silent for a long while. 'Y'know, Poll, I think maybe we'll run away and get married in England. Bugger all parents.'

'Is Grandpa being a domestic tyrant?'

'No. I don't really think so. I think he has a point. So, I think, does Katie, but she doesn't want to upset her mother.'

'She's very young.'

He laughed. 'Well, she's older than you, at any rate.'

'I don't think I'd care about upsetting my mother, not if I was really in love with someone.' I felt brave saying the words, grown up, as if I knew what I was talking about. 'What were you going to do about it before Grandpa brought the subject up?'

'We hadn't even discussed it. I think we both hoped it might never arise. Don't mention it, don't ask anyone about it, leave it alone and it will go away. Typical lethargical Protestant attitude. At least on my part.'

'You could just sign the bit of paper and then forget about it.'

'No, darling. Not possible. You can't start a whole life with someone by swearing an oath you have no intention of keeping. Not good, that, not good at all.'

It was getting dark now, evening drawing on, and lights were flickering on in the houses we could see from the road. We turned right in Kilcolgan and the road became narrow and winding, the surface coated with leaves blown from the trees by the damp west wind.

'But you never told me how they are,' I said after a while.

'And you never told me whether you know where Sam is or not.'

'How can I tell you what I don't know?'

He shook his head.

I wanted to tell him what I knew. I wanted badly to tell someone, disburden myself, but I suppose I didn't trust him. Even if he didn't say a word to his parents he would tell Katie, and she would tell her parents and so on and on and soon the whole world would know and it would all be my fault.

He touched my shoulder gently. 'It's OK, Polly . . . I shouldn't be ballyragging you like this. I'm just in a bit of a stew about everything at the moment.'

'I'm sorry.'

'Perhaps we should go and live in England. Maybe. We are talking about it.'

'You couldn't. Honestly. Think about the old dears and Kildarragh. What would happen to it? And what would happen to you in England? What would you do? I think it's a rotten idea.'

'Hush. Calm down. We're just talking at the moment. Considering options. And you're not to say a word. Not a word . . . to anyone.'

'Why do people always—' I shut my mouth tight. 'Think of them.' I whispered the words.

I don't know whether he heard me or not, but we drove for the next twenty minutes or so in an uneasy silence. The rain rattled on the windscreen, sounding like pebbles thrown in great handfuls by the wind and dashing against the car.

'It's been like this for a week now. A bit depressing,' he said.

I didn't answer. I think that wrapped in the warmth of the rug I must have fallen asleep because the next thing I knew we were bumping up the avenue in thick darkness.

'There must be a power failure,' he said. 'I haven't seen a light for miles.'

'We're home,' I said happily, forgetting all the problems in my head.

'Yup, Baby, home it is.' He gave a little triumphant toot on the horn and stopped the car. The house was black, except for a flickering glow that shone out through the fanlight over the front door. The rain was easing off, the wind coming in little spurts from the direction of the sea, carrying with it the ocean smell I loved so much, salty and with a hint of turf smoke. I stood breathing it in.

'Move, Polly, move. You'll freeze if you stand there.'

The hall door opened and Grandma stood there, silhouetted by the candlelight.

'Come quickly, dear children, otherwise all the candles in the house will blow out and then we will be like Moses in the dark.'

I ran into her welcoming arms, Harry following with my case. She pulled me into the hall and closed the door.

'What a night, and no electricity to boot. Harry, darling, have you candles? Sadie said I must ask you that very important question. She is sure you won't have any and says I must give you some, just to get you through the night. They're on the table.'

'As usual, Sadie is right. Good evening, Mama. I've brought you a precious parcel from Dublin and I must fly away as I'm eating with the Whelans. Goodnight, Polly. I'll see you tomorrow. Sleep well. Thank Sadie for the candles. Love to Father.' He picked up a pile of candles from the hall table and was gone before we could say anything.

'Thank you for the lift,' I called, but the door had closed behind him.

One of the girls had lit the fire in my bedroom and shadows leapt and tumbled on the walls. I hung up my coat and brushed my hair and went out on to the landing to go to the bathroom and wash my hands for dinner. Grandpa was standing at the top of the stairs; he stretched out his arms when he saw me.

'Jassie. My darling Jassie. You have come home. My darling girl.'

'Grandpa, I'm not—' At that moment the lights came on.

We stood blinking at each other, he at the top of the stairs, me a little bit down the passage that led to my bedroom. I didn't know what to say. He stared. From down the stairs Grandma's voice could be heard calling.

'Glory be to God on high. We have light. All candles out. Now. At once. We must preserve the candles for next time.'

Grandpa put both his hands up to his face and rubbed at his eyes. 'Of course,' he muttered. 'Of course.'

I heard her feet patter to the bottom of the stairs. 'Geoffrey? Geoffrey, did you hear me?'

'No.' He almost whispered the word. 'No. Hear? No. No. It's Polly.'

I put my arm around his thin shoulders; he was shaking. I pulled him gently towards the library.

'Come, Grandpa darling, we'll blow out the candles in your room. That's what Grandma wants us to do. Then we'll go down and have dinner.'

'I thought you were . . .'

'Yes, I know. I'm sorry.'

'Polly.' It was Grandma calling. 'Is everything all right?'

'Yes, fine. We just had a little problem. Everything's all right now. We'll be down in a few minutes.'

All the lights were blazing in the library; he sank into his big chair, looking exhausted. I poured him a small tot of whisky from the bottle on his desk and handed it to him. He drank it down in one go.

'I'm sorry, Baby . . . I hope I didn't frighten you. I have frightened myself, indeed I have. I seem to be slipping, and I don't want to slip. I just want to die, not to wake up one morning. I really don't want to slip. I loved her so much, that one. My girl. And I never cried a tear for her.' He took my hand and held it to his cheek, his rutted and raddled cheek. 'Bloody war. Never cried a bloody tear. I cried for that dog. That's the stupidity of man, isn't it? Your grandmother came in to my room and found me sitting beside the poor old dog on the rug, and I was crying. She put her arms around me and she laughed and then I started to laugh too. You won't ever go to war, will you?'

'No.'

'That's a girl. Let's go down and have dinner and don't you dare tell your grandmother what a fool I've been.' I helped him up and we went downstairs. She looked carefully at us both as we arrived in the dining room but never asked a question. The lights flickered from time to time, but remained with us for the rest of the evening.

Later that night as I lay curled in my warm bed, watching the fire turning in on itself and dying in the grate, the door opened and Grandma's head appeared.

'Are you asleep?'

'No.'

She came in and shut the door quietly behind her. 'I

just wondered what had happened. You know, before dinner. You don't have to tell me if you don't want to. I just wondered.' I sat up. She was standing in the middle of the room in her dressing gown with her hair in a long plait hanging over her right shoulder.

'He thought I was Jassie.'

'Ah.'

'And then when the lights came on he saw I wasn't. That was all. He didn't want you to know.'

'The poor old darling.' She stood for a moment in the middle of the room and then turned without another word and left, closing the door quietly behind her. I lay wondering whether her last remark was referring to her dead daughter or her live husband.

✳   ✳   ✳

My five days with them passed in a flash; the rain disappeared and the whole countryside was orange and blue and the sea was covered with sparkling waves and the smell of turf smoke rose from every chimney and I rode my pony down to the beach and along the edge of the sea and felt well and loved. Fires were lit and crackled in the grates and spat red sparks out on to the hearth rugs, leaving little black holes. 'One night the whole place will go up in smoke, if the master goes on buying that old cracky wood from Paddy Deery,' grumbled Sadie. She had being saying the same thing for years and the house was still standing. Grandpa said from time to time that he didn't think that Paddy Deery had any vested interest in burning the house to the ground and he would continue to buy wood from him no matter what Sadie thought. The evenings I spent reading in the library, jumping up from time to time to kill any sparks that flew from the fire, with my wetted fingers, before they could burn their tiny black holes in the rug. 'Bravo, Polly,' Grandpa would say without lifting his eyes from whatever book he might be reading. We could hear the sound of Grandma playing the piano drifting up through the floor, and sometimes she might sing, mostly Schubert, to whom she was greatly attached, but occasionally she would burst into 'Oh I do like to be beside the seaside, I do like to be beside the sea. I do like to stroll upon the prom prom prom where the brass bands play tiddley-om-pom-pom . . . I do like to be beside the sea.' She would shout tiddley-om-pom-pom loudly, to make sure we heard her, and Grandpa would murmur, 'Oh, that tiddley-om-pom woman,' again without raising his eyes from whatever he was reading. I loved the peace of those evenings.

Mrs Whelan telephoned to ask us to dinner.

'We'll be three,' Grandma said. 'Polly's here. Will that be all right?' and Mrs Whelan must have said it would. Grandma put down the receiver and shouted up the stairs. 'Tuesday evening, Geoffrey, we're having dinner with the Whelans.'

The door of his room burst open. 'What was that you said?'

'Dinner with the Whelans.'

'Why?' He sounded like some huge dying animal mourning his ill-spent life. 'Why oh why?'

'Don't be silly, darling. You know perfectly well why.'

'Polly can go instead of me.'

'Polly is going as well as you.'

'Maybe I will be rude to them.'

'No you bloody well won't. You'll be an angel of sweetness and light. You like them, you know you do. Think of poor Harry and just behave yourself. Nothing contentious will be said.'

He fixed his eyes on me. 'Where is Sam?'

'Grandpa . . .'

'Leave her alone, Geoffrey. She has told us, she hasn't the faintest idea.'

'And what's more you are too big for that pony. Beatrice, we must get the girl another horse. A horse, not that little itty-bitty thing she goes hacking around on at the moment.'

'I like Benjy.'

'You'll kill him. You're too big to be riding him. He's a child's pony. You're not a child any longer. Don't worry. He won't go to the knacker. He'll live a life of quietude eating good meadow grass. Heavenly retirement. The next time you come down you will have a proper horse.'

❊   ❊   ❊

'Of course you know Jassie?' were Grandpa's first words to Mrs Whelan.

I put out my hand to shake hers and at the same time said out loud and quite clearly, 'Polly. I'm Polly.'

'Of course I know Polly.' She leant forward and kissed me on the cheek. 'Though, my goodness, she's grown up since I saw her last. Come in out of the cold.'

She hustled us into the hall and closed the door behind us. She was a pretty woman, neat and nicely scented; a perfect doctor's wife, I thought to myself, sympathetic and considerate. There was an ornate cross hanging round her neck and I did wonder for a moment if this was to protect her from Grandpa's intemperate words; I pushed the thought quickly from my mind. Grandma looked tense; she was holding Grandpa's arm in a grip of iron. He had a faint smile on his face.

Everyone behaved impeccably until the pudding was brought in, a delicious-looking *mousse au chocolat*. Grandpa dipped his spoon and sat looking at it for a moment, and then he smiled.

'Of course,' he said, 'there is no need for this wedding—'

'Geoffrey,' said Grandma.

'— to be in a Roman church, is there? Then there would be no need—'

'Geoffrey!'

'— for this bit of paper to be signed, would there?'

Dr Whelan coughed. Mrs Whelan put her spoon down carefully on her plate.

'I presume we all are agreed on the venality of this bit of paper. You are intelligent people. It seems to me to be some kind of spiritual blackmail.'

'I have spoken to the bishop.'

He paid her no heed. 'The Church of Ireland is quite respectable. I imagine that God smiles as favourably on its members as on all the others, wherever they may say their prayers. It would be a strange thing if he didn't, wouldn't it?'

'Father,' said Harry. 'Enough.'

'The bishop is adamant.'

'You are lucky to have an adamant bishop. I would speak to my bishop if I thought he would do anything except whinge.'

'Eat up your pudding, Geoffrey, then we must go.'

'My dear Beatrice, this is an important matter. It is to do with freedom. I know you believe in freedom. So do we all. I believe that. So why do we let our young be bullied by the old and old-fashioned? I have no prejudice against my grandchildren becoming Romans if they so wish, none at all, but I do have a prejudice against their being coerced or bullied. Harry, stop making faces at me. I will be allowed to speak. You can tear me apart when we get home, Beatrice. That is your right. I have now my right to speak. And you all have the right to pay no attention to me. We all have rights, and no one, be he priest or bishop or the Pope himself, has got the right to take those rights away from us. I fought for freedom. So did you, Harry.' He put the spoonful of mousse into his mouth and sat back. He looked at Grandma. 'Am I a domestic tyrant?'

She shook her head.

'Yes you are,' said Harry. 'I believe you are. You have become one. This is my life, my marriage, and you are daring to interfere. If that's not being a tyrant I don't know what is. This is my problem you're talking about; my possible children.'

'I'm talking about freedom. That's all, pure and simple.' He tottered to his feet and held his glass in the air. 'Freedom.' He collapsed once more into his chair. He took a large mouthful of wine and swished it round the inside of his mouth before swallowing it. Dr Whelan mopped his forehead with his napkin, his lips looking very tightly zipped together. Mrs Whelan's face was red.

'Freedom.' There was a sob in his voice as he repeated the word.

Grandma picked up her bag from the floor; she pushed back her chair and stood up.

'Come, dearests, we must go home. Yes, the time has come. Get your coat, Polly. Geoffrey, you have upset everyone enough for one evening. Come, rise up now and we'll go.' She smiled her charming smile at the Whelans. 'Forgive us, my dears. All will be well, you'll see. All will be well. All manner of things.' She turned abruptly and left the room. I ran over to Grandpa, who was sitting looking moodily into his glass, and put my hand under his elbow.

'Where's Beatrice gone?'

'Come on, Grandpa darling. She's outside.'

'I haven't finished my pudding. Which, I must say, is simply delicious.' He bowed towards Mrs Whelan.

I pulled at his arm, but he remained seated. Harry stood up.

'I'll drive you home, Father. I think it would be best.'

Katie clutched at him. 'Don't go, Harry. Please.'

Gently he removed her hand from his sleeve. 'I'll be back. Straight back. This is all ridiculous, darling. I'll just drop them home and I'll come straight back. Father is not well.'

Grandpa pulled himself to his feet, using me as a lever. He straightened his back to its full extent. 'Jassie will drive.' He patted my shoulder.

Harry laughed. 'Polly is only sixteen. She can't drive.'

'I taught her myself. She learnt with more ease than any of you boys. During the war . . .' He stopped talking and moved slowly towards the door. 'Beatrice!' He strode out of the room, Harry on his heels. I looked at the Whelans: Dr Whelan was on his feet and his wife was fumbling in her pockets for a handkerchief.

'Um, sorry,' I said. 'Grandpa's not . . . well. He's just having a little turn. I'm sorry . . . hope . . . um . . . thank you. Yes. Thank you very much. Lovely dinner.' I dashed out of the room.

It was raining, soft wetting rain that stuck on your hair and clothes. We ran to the car and I clambered into the back and Harry pushed his father in after me.

'Jassie . . .'

'Polly. I'm Polly.'

'Yes, of course you are. I just call you Jassie from time to time. My lovely Jassie. Did you know her?'

'Geoffrey dearest, do stop this nonsense. You know quite well that—'

Harry slammed the front door and turned on the engine, then leant forward and rubbed at the windscreen with his hand.

'Father,' he said, 'you have said quite enough for one evening.'

'Truth,' said Grandpa. 'I have spoken my truth. And look what happens.' He took hold of my hand and brought it to his lips. 'Jassie,' he said and fell asleep.

Harry drove off quite fast and we all remained silent until we got back to Kildarragh. He stopped the car at the bottom of the steps, got out and opened all the doors for us. His face was pale and stiff.

'I'll bring back the car first thing in the morning. Good night, Mother.' He kissed Grandma and got back into his seat and slammed the door. Grandma sighed as she watched the car disappear down the avenue. She tucked her arm through Grandpa's and they began to walk slowly up the steps, and heavily, I thought as I watched them; their steps sounded like the steps of really old people. I wanted to peel off years; I wanted them to be once more in their prime of life.

'I hope,' she was saying to him, 'that you haven't put a big killer cat among those pigeons.' He laughed, a laugh a bit like a sob, I thought. He put out a hand and opened the door and the pair of them went into the hall.

'I wouldn't do that, would I?' His voice was anxious. 'I have never wanted to be a pigeon slayer.' They walked across the hall to the drawing room, where the lights were on and the curtains pulled and I could hear the crackling of the logs in the fire; Sadie always seemed to know what was the right thing to do. I went to bed and for a long time I heard the rising and falling of their voices drifting up through the floor, sometimes just a level murmur and sometimes Grandma's voice sharp, penetrating, and then sinking once more to its reasonable norm.

I was dressed and packed by eight thirty. I really didn't want to go. I wanted to know how things would turn out and I didn't want to go back to Sandymount, school or even Nonie, but I knew there was little point in asking if I could stay. I bumped my case down the stairs and left it in the hall. There was the most wonderful smell of bacon drifting in the air. In the dining room Grandma was eating porridge and reading a letter and Grandpa, at the other end of the table, had hidden himself behind the *Irish Times*. Grandma put her letter down when I came into the room.

'Polly darling, I have asked Mr Riordan to drive you to the station. There's no sign yet of Harry with the car and anyway I'm feeling a little worn. I do hope you don't mind. I just feel a long drive like that would wear me out completely. There's lovely porridge, dear, and Sadie has made eggs and bacon and all sorts of other deliciousnesses to see you through. No letter from Sam. He is such a bad boy.'

I helped myself to porridge; outside the weather was fierce, a gale blowing the rain against the windows and the leaves in colourful waves across the lawn. I put my plate on the table and quietly crept round behind Grandpa's chair. I placed my hands on his shoulders and kissed him on the top of his head. He didn't turn round, but caught one of my hands in his.

'Whoever you are, I am in bad odour. You kiss me at your peril.'

I kissed him again. In return he kissed my hand.

'Bad odour.'

'This is another day, Geoffrey. We all smell as sweet as new mown hay. Polly, eat your porridge while it is hot. Mr Riordan will be here at ten.'

'It's nice to have her round the place. Why do you have to go, my dear?'

'I have school and all that stuff. I'd much rather be here.'

'There's Nonie, and the little ones. You mustn't forget them. We're not the only family she has.'

We heard the front door bang and footsteps crossing the hall. The door opened and Harry came in. He stood looking at us for a moment before speaking.

'Ah, breakfast.' He walked across the room and sat down at the table. He looked wretched. 'Get me some porridge, Polly, there's a girl. And coffee please, Mother, black.'

Grandpa threw the paper on to the floor and stared across the table at his son. 'Well?'

I wondered what he meant by the grunted word.

Harry put his hand into his coat pocket and took out something which he threw across the table towards his father. It rolled clumsily through the cups and saucers, the knives and forks, the breakfast accoutrements; it was the ring he had given Katie not all that many weeks before.

'You've won.'

Grandpa picked the ring up and looked at it and then placed it back on the table. 'Won?' he asked.

I put Harry's porridge down in front of him and went back to my chair.

'Yes, Father. I am no longer engaged to Katie. She has given me the ring back.'

Grandpa looked bewildered. 'I don't understand . . .' He picked up the ring again and turned it in his fingers, staring fixedly down at it.

'Yes,' he said after a long silence. 'That ring belonged to my mama.' He tried pushing the ring on to a finger, but even though his fingers were thin and bony he couldn't push it down below the first joint. 'She had such small hands, tiny, such slim fingers, and yet she played the piano with such . . . Do you remember, Beatrice?'

'Yes, my darling, I do indeed.'

'Strength . . . and grace.' He turned to Harry. 'I don't

understand. What possible reason could she have had for giving you back the ring?'

'Her mother was very upset by your little exhibition last night.'

'I wasn't talking to her mother. I was merely expressing my opinion. I was talking to the world at large. I am allowed to do that, here in my own country, in my own bloody neck of the woods.'

'You upset her mother.'

'Mrs Whelan is a charming and intelligent woman.'

'Geoffrey . . .'

Harry waved his spoon at his father and little slops of porridge splashed on to the table.

'Oh, Harry, do watch out.' Grandma patted at the splashes with her napkin. Her voice sounded thick and I wondered if she were going to cry.

'A charming and intelligent woman.' Grandpa repeated the words, louder than before. 'I do not see why—'

'Don't be absurd, Father. You know perfectly well why she's upset. She is a good, devout Catholic. Her family is coming down with priests, young and old. There's a monsignor and two canons. She does good work, she believes what the Church tells her. She loves her daughter.'

'So?'

'She worries about the souls of the unborn.'

'Oh, for the love of God . . .' Grandpa pushed his chair back and stamped across the room, leaving the ring on the table. He slammed the door behind him and I could hear his footsteps beating across the hall and slowly climbing the stairs.

Grandma stretched a hand out across the table and touched Harry's arm. 'Tell me what happened.'

He clutched at her hand. Age seemed to have slipped away from him and he looked like a forlorn small boy. I held my breath.

'Well, I went straight back last night. I couldn't have been more then fifteen minutes, twenty perhaps, and they were still sitting in the dining room, dishes, pudding and all still there. No Katie, though.'

'Where was she?'

'Gone. Just gone. No one said. No one mentioned her. The doctor just sat there and looked grey. She spoke and he nodded his head from time to time. She asked me if I realised how young Katie was, how impressionable. Did I realise, she said, how she had been protected from every possible bad and evil thing that could happen in the world, by her school, by her mother, by the Church, and did I not wish as her parents did that she could live for ever with such protection? I didn't say a word, not a word. The doctor just looked at the floor. Having said what she wanted to say there was a very long pause and then she said, "I didn't realise that your father hated Catholics." I shook my head. Words wouldn't come out of my mouth, they sort of got stuck. We sat there for an age in total silence. Then she said, "Well?" "I don't think he does," I said. "I think he got a bit carried away. No. In fact definitely no. I apologise if he upset you. He didn't mean to." I was sorry I'd said that. It just sort of came out. I felt a rat having apologised on Father's behalf when ... when ...'

Grandma stroked his fingers. 'Darling boy ... everything will be all right. Just wait and see.' She sounded doubtful. 'Eat your breakfast, Polly, or you'll have Sadie after you. And keep an eye on the time. You mustn't miss your train. Harry ...'

'The next thing she said was, "Of course you'll be

taking instructions. I spoke to the bishop about that the other day." And I said no. No instructions, thank you, Mrs Whelan, I will not be taking instructions. She took the ring from her pocket and put it on the table. She pushed it towards me. I didn't touch it. "I gave it to Katie; I'll take it back from her. Where is she? She should be here." "You're saying no?" The doctor coughed then and got to his feet. Poor bloke, I feel quite sorry for him. He walked over to the window and stood there with his hands in his pockets, jingling stuff . . . you know, keys and stuff. God, I do hope Father doesn't leave him. Anyway, I said "I want to see Katie" and she said "Are you saying yes or no?" and I said, "No." Just like that: quite calmly, no shouting, no hysterics, "No." She got up from her chair and came over to me and pushed the ring into my hand. "I gave her the choice," she said. "I told her that she can go with you and never see us again, her family who love her, who want to keep her from all harm. She can throw us away, phttt, like that, and the faith she has grown up with, that has protected her all these years, she can throw that away as well. The Church loves her too. Or she can stay with us. There are plenty of good men in the world. She doesn't have to marry you. She doesn't have to marry away from us all, throw us away like so much rubbish. Oh, no."'

Grandma interrupted him. 'Listen to me, my son, my dear son. You've had a horrible experience, I won't deny that, all created by Geoffrey, I won't deny that either, but all he did was speed the whole thing up. This would have happened anyway, you may be sure of that. She had already spoken to the bishop, she said so. My advice is let the hare sit. Sit and sit. Have patience. Katie will come to you. She's a nice sensible girl; she won't put up with this sort of nonsense from her mother.'

'I wouldn't,' I said, I thought helpfully. Grandma shook her head at me; she obviously didn't agree. I went over to the sideboard and helped myself to eggs and bacon. Their voices were low behind me.

'She and her mother are very close.'

'She and you are very close.'

'I think I love her more than she loves me. I think she's a bit dazzled by my . . . oh, I don't know what, just my being so devoted to her . . . Oh, Mother.'

'Let the hare sit,' she said again. She picked up the ring and held it out to him. 'Put this away safely, son.

I've no doubt you will be needing it again. Now, Polly. Eat up quickly, dear girl. Mr Riordan will be here soon.'

'I don't want to go,' I muttered to my plate. Nobody else seemed to hear me. 'Why,' I asked aloud, perhaps even louder than aloud so that they would listen, 'do families have to fight? Why do they have to hurt each other's feelings? That's what I would like to know.'

'No need to shout, dear. We all say things that other people don't agree with, things that other people don't want to hear. The thing about families is that we're not saying I don't love you to the other person, simply I don't agree with you. We all have to give each other space for agreeing and disagreeing. Sometimes feelings get too easily hurt.' She poured herself another cup of tea. 'I do hope that Geoffrey will calm down. He's overheated at the moment. It isn't good for him.'

'Grandma, you told me that love abideth for ever. Is that true?'

'Baby, will you for God's sake eat your breakfast and shut up.'

'Leave her be, Harry. She's going soon, then you must go to bed and sleep for a while. You look as if you haven't closed your eyes all night. Some other time, Polly dear, we'll talk about love everlasting and a lot of other stuff like that. Now why on earth did I pour myself out that cup of tea?' The door bell rattled. 'That must be Mr Riordan. Scoot, dear girl. Go and say your goodbyes. Tell Grandpa that I'll be up in a few minutes.'

I went up to Grandpa's room and opened the door. He was standing by the window, staring out at the fields and the distant sea.

'Ah, Jassie,' he said. 'I presume you've come to say goodbye.'

'I'm afraid so.' I went over and put my arms around his neck and kissed his scratchy cheek and he put his arms around me and we stood together and stared out at the fields, where three horses cropped the grass peacefully and the sun made sparks on the sea beyond. Below us on the avenue Sadie was talking to Mr Riordan.

'I'm afraid so too,' Grandpa murmured. 'You go away too often, my dear.'

'I'll be back. I promise. You take care of yourself.'

He was shaking. I disentangled his arms from round me and kissed him again.

'Beatrice will take care of me. Goodbye, dear Jassie, and don't get killed again.' He turned back to the fields and the sea and I slipped out of the room.

Grandma was in the hall. 'Give Nonie my love, and those sweet little ones, and come back as soon as you can. You know we love having you here.' She hugged me and gave me a quick push towards the door. 'Everything will be all right, you'll see. I must fly up to my dear old man and give him a piece of my mind. Travel safely.'

She was gone across the hall and quickly up the stairs. She was crying, I was crying, Grandpa was crying, Harry was crying, was Sadie crying? I hated all these tears. This was my happy place. I wanted it to remain my happy place. Damn all these salt tears.

Mr Riordan was holding the back door of the car open for me.

'Can't I go in front?'

'Get in and behave like the grown-up young lady that you are,' Sadie murmured low in my ear. Then she shoved a box into my hand and gave me an enormous hug. 'That's something to keep you going on that long old journey. Mr Riordan will put your case on the train for you. See you soon. I'll mind them well, and Harry too. We'll all mind poor Harry. Bye now, Polly.'

I got into the car, clutching my box. 'Goodbye, Sadie, and thanks.'

Mr Riordan closed the door and I sat alone and waved, not feeling grown up at all, but I supposed that I must be nearly there.

As we jolted down the avenue I looked out of the back window and I could see Grandpa standing alone, almost desolate, in the window of his room.

'I hear it round that the general's not too well these days?'

'Why do you call him the general? He's not a general.'

'I don't know. He's always been the general as far as I can remember. Didn't he have has leg blown off in that terrible war and didn't he come back like so many didn't and hasn't he been here with us always? No more decent man. Liked by one and all. We don't like to hear of him not being well.'

'He's just getting old, Mr Riordan. He takes little turns, but he'll be all right. I'm sure . . . I hope. I do hope.'

I settled back into the seat; it was a long journey to my other life.

Nonie met me at the station, with the two little ones in the back of the car. To my surprise I was really pleased to see them. We did a lot of hugging and kissing before Nonie shut the car door and said, 'Home, James.' In the few days that I had been away Sue had learnt a song, which she proceeded to sing for us, Shane throwing in his tuppence worth when he felt like it.

'Daisy, Daisy, give me your answer do. I'm half crazy, all for the love of you.'

'Give me do.'

'It won't be a stylish marriage.'

'Arriage.'

'We can't afford a carriage. But you'd look sweet—'

'Sweet.'

'— upon the seat of a bicycle made for two.'

'Bikell for two. Sweet. Mummy, sweet.'

'That's very good, Susie. Who taught you that?'

'Daddy. He played the piano and I sang.'

'And me sing. Sweet, Mummy. Bikell for two. Sweet, Mummy.'

'Mummy is busy driving and can't give you a sweet now, darling.'

'Sweeeeet,' he roared. His sister pushed him, not very gently. He kicked her, and then fell off the seat. Susie started roaring.

'Mummy, he kicked me. He really hurt me. Oooooh.'

'Welcome home,' said Nonie to me.

'Ooooh.' Sue threw herself down on to Shane and began to pull his hair. He began to cry, real tears.

'Stop. Stop this minute. Susie, leave him alone.' Nonie swung over to the kerb and stopped the car. She turned round and glared at the two children; she took hold of Sue's shoulder and pulled her away from Shane.

'Shane, now, get up, climb over into the front and sit on Polly's knee. How can I be expected to drive the car with you two carrying on like this? Shut up, Susie, you're behaving like a baby.'

'He kicked me.'

'No Polly's knee. NO.'

'Now, Shane, now. Do what you're told. Shut up, Susie.'

'Boo hoo. Boo hoo.' My voice was so loud that everyone turned and stared at me.

'Now what on earth is the matter with you?' said Nonie.

'Boo hoo. I want Shane to sit on my knee. I shall boo and hoo until he does.'

He climbed on to the back of the seat. 'Silly Polly,' he said. 'Silly billy Polly.' He tumbled over on to my knee and leant his face against mine. 'Shane love Polly.'

The car started once more.

'Polly love Shane.'

✳   ✳   ✳

There was a letter for me on the hall table; I recognised Marcus's scrawl. I grabbed it and shoved it into my pocket. Nonie raised her eyebrows at me and I pretended not to see.

'How are they?' she asked as soon as we were sitting down and the children had gone into the kitchen to have their supper with the au pair girl.

'OK.'

'What does that mean?'

'It means OK. Fine. They're fine. Grandpa's going to buy me a new pony. We had a blackout. No lights for miles around. Spooky. Nothing new really. Everyone's OK. They're getting old. I hate that.'

'When's the wedding going to be?'

'I don't know. We didn't talk about it, or not a lot anyway. Harry wasn't there much. That's why they like me being there, otherwise they'd be . . .' I stopped. I didn't know if I wanted to say any more.

'Be what?'

'On their own.'

'You mustn't be silly about them, Polly. You mustn't think that you are responsible for them; you're not, darling. They have lots of people to look after them. They're quite safe, and when Harry gets married there'll be one more person to keep an eye on them. You have a life of your own.'

I didn't want to say anything, so I sat, mute, each move I made crackling the envelope in my pocket. She sighed.

'Stretching ahead . . . lots of wonderful life. Let the old fade gracefully away. They've had their day. Does that sound unkind? I didn't mean it to, it's just that I wouldn't want you to get too involved in all that dismal County Clare life. The world has more to offer than that.'

'I love County Clare.'

'It's OK for holidays.'

'You don't know what it's like. You don't know the people, the sea, the landscape, the way it smells, the birds in the early morning, the wind from the ocean. Nothing. You've hardly ever been there, only short little stays with Daddy. You couldn't know it. You couldn't understand.' I got up and ran from the room and up the stairs to my bedroom. I slammed the door; I thought that might make me feel better, but it didn't. I lay on my bed in the almost dark and watched the shadows cast on the ceiling by the street lights outside. I wanted to cry, to bawl out loud about the fact that I was lonely, that I wanted Sadie and the big black range at Kildarragh, I needed to be understood and comforted and loved by everyone around me. Lights moved and streaked the ceiling and the purring and grinding of the cars passing outside on the road sounded like jungle animals on the prowl. I knew I was being foolish; I was behaving like a spoiled adolescent, a despised adolescent. I shifted my body and the letter crackled in my pocket and I remembered it. I sat up and switched on the light and pulled the envelope out. I opened it: there was only one page inside, no note from Sam.

Dear Polly,

My mother is, as usual, throwing a big bash for Hogmanay (that is New Year to all nonsensical non-Scots). We all wondered if you would like to come and stay for it. It is usually quite fun: dancing and all that sort of stuff. I am almost the eldest of a long line of kilt wearers so there will be plenty of young sprigs and sprogs for you to enjoy yourself with. Should my mama write to your mother, or will this do as a formal invitation? We are well brought up and pretty harmless so there should be no fear for your safety. I do look forward to seeing you.

Marcus

PS Oh frabjous day, I go to Paris in January, to learn and work and become great and famous. Don't you think this is worth a celebration? It would be so nice if you could come and I will meet you at the airport whenever you decide to arrive.

I jumped off my bed and flew down the stairs.
'Nonie. Nonie. Nonie.'

'Darling, what is it? I'm in the kitchen.'

She was putting away the children's supper dishes
when I went in. I held the letter out towards her.

'I've been invited to a party. Please say yes, Nonie,
please, please.'

She smiled; she took the letter from my hand and I
watched her reading it. As she read she curled a strand
of her hair round and round her finger.

'I don't see why not,' she said at last. 'We'll ask
Charles what he thinks.'

Why Charles? I asked inside my head. It was
what she and I thought that mattered; nothing to do
with Charles. Nothing at all. I didn't speak such
thoughts out loud, though. I had more sense. Anyway,
what with one thing and another they said I could
go. Marcus's mother would write to them and they
would arrange the travelling problems between then.
I would go on a plane from Dublin to Edinburgh;
that in itself was pretty exciting, and I would stay
at home for Christmas and not grumble and Nonie
would take me into town and we would buy a lovely

Hogmanay dress, so no one could talk about the poor shabby Irish.

I wrote to Marcus.

Dear Marcus,

I am so looking forward to your party; thank you so much for inviting me. I have never been out of the country before, I have never been in an aeroplane before, I have never been to a real grown-up party before, so taken all in all the prospect is very exciting.

Thank you again and again.

I didn't mention Sam. I wanted to; my fingers itched to write his name. Each night in my dreaming I saw him in the halls and drawing rooms of great Scottish castles, at the bend of a curving stone staircase or standing by a tall window staring out at mountains grey and wet with mist. Sam, I would call out each time I saw him, and would wake myself up and find myself nowhere more exciting than my Sandymount bedroom, with the yellow sodium lights outside in the street and the hill of Howth across the black bay. I did remain good-humoured, though. I smiled, I minded the small ones, I read them stories and took them for the odd run on the beach when the tide was out. I did my homework and helped with the washing-up, a model daughter; and Nonie took me to Brown Thomas one afternoon and we bought the most beautiful dress that I had ever seen, of deep rosy-coloured silk with a little velvet jacket to match, because of the cold in Scotland, and a pair of black velvet dancing shoes with glittering silver buckles. Such finery. Such excitement inside my belly, my lungs, my heart.

Not a word from Sam, and when Grandma telephoned me on Christmas Day the first thing she said was, 'Have you heard from Sam?'

'No.'

'Oh, dearie me. Neither have we. Listen, dear child, you don't think anything awful has—'

'No, Grandma, he's just being bad. Don't worry. Please, darling, don't worry.'

'You know something?'

'No. I promise.' I crossed my fingers. 'I promise. Not a squeak.' My hands were shaking.

'Mmm.' I could feel her disbelief coming down the line at me.

'How's Grandpa?'

'The boys are all here.'

'And Katie?'

'No. Just the boys. We miss you, darling.'

'And Grandpa? You never told me how he is.'

'He's not exactly brimming with Christmas spirit. That's a joke. He's all right. Very silent. He doesn't seem to like talking any more. He spends most of his time in the library, just sitting, staring at the fire. He misses that damn dog. Come down soon.' She snapped the receiver down and that was that. I hadn't had time to tell her about my invitation. I hadn't been able to speak to the dear old man. Neither of us had said happy Christmas to the other. I felt gloom wrapping itself round me.

I felt gloom really all over Christmas, until, in fact, I sat strapped into my seat on the plane to Edinburgh; then my heart began to beat with such excitement that I thought it might explode. It was a bright clear day, not a cloud in the sky and a biting frost. I glued my face to the window and stared down mesmerised by the lines of the land and sea. We had a map at school which showed the contours of Ireland, the hills, mountains, rivers, bogs and plains all surrounded by the wrinkled blue-grey of the sea, but from up here, higher even than a bird could fly, or an angel, it looked better still. I thought about angels for a while as I watched the pattern of the land and sea below me, bright under the sun; I could see shimmering long lines of sunlight on sweeping waves. It was definitely better than the map at school; it was alive. As we approached the English coast small white clouds flew with us in the sky, or perhaps they were angels, their white puffy wings spreading in the wind, bearing them up, racing us. And then there was snow and the land underneath us was white and green, and mountains gathered with their rocks and trees. It was amazing, and I thought to myself that when I grew up I would be a pilot, so that every day I could be a part of this adventure with the world and the air and elements.

* * *

Marcus was there, standing taller than the rest by the gate. He looked sombre, but when he saw me he smiled a huge welcoming smile. He put both arms around me and bumped the top of my head with his chin.

'Marvellous, Polly. There you are. Pretty as a picture. Did you have a wonderful flight? I'm so happy to see you. Give me that case. We have to dash, I'm afraid, no wandering round Edinburgh. The weather's not going to be kind, so we must try to be home before dark.' He took my hand into the crook of his elbow. 'And I am most illegally parked. Most. Speed is of the essence.'

We sped, paying no attention to any thing or person until we arrived panting at a jeep-like vehicle parked half on and half off the pathway just outside the door of the main airport building. The car was un-locked. 'In you hop.' I opened the door and hopped in and he threw my bag on to the back seat and hopped in himself and we were off without any delay. The moment we had turned on to the main road he relaxed back into his seat, patted my hand and smiled that big smile again.

'Now,' he said, 'now you can talk. Blather on, Poll. I hope I haven't exhausted you with all that running, but I hate damn bloody airports and all the nonsense they go on with. In and out is what you need, just in and out. No hanging around. I'm so glad you're here.' He leant dangerously towards me and kissed the top of my head again.

'Hello, Marcus,' I said finally. 'Hello, hello, hello. I've never been out of Ireland before, so I'm a little stunned . . . and breathless. Hello.'

'Hello. Welcome.'

'Hello,' I said again, and then for some reason or other I burst into tears.

'Hey.' He pulled the car over to the kerb and stopped. 'Baby.' He put his arms round me and hugged me. 'What's this?'

'You know, I never really thought I would get away. I could never see that far ahead. I felt I was going to be there for ever. Trundling between Dublin and Kildarragh. That was my world until today. I feel tearfully excited. Sorry.'

'No need for sorry. Have my handkerchief. Here. Mop up and we'll start off again.' I mopped and he gently edged the car back out into the traffic and we headed out of the city.

He seemed to need to talk. We ate up the miles and the daylight; all around the landscape became more and more white and from time to time I could feel the wheels slipping under us.

'I'm a good driver, you know. There's no need for you to be frightened.'

'I'm not frightened,' I lied. He grinned at me, and did a sideways swoop.

'We won't be long now. Tell me about Kildarragh. How are things there, and your lovely grandparents? I hope they're well.'

I told him about Harry and Katie's brief engagement and Pluto's death and Grandpa's failing health and the words flowed out of my mouth like water from an open tap and he listened gravely, until he swung suddenly off the road between high gateposts topped with stags' heads. He stopped the car by the avenue's edge and took my hands in his.

'We'll talk more about this. We're almost home. I promise we'll have undisturbed talk. There are things I want . . . I have to say to you . . .'

'About Sam?'

We turned a corner and I saw the house across the white fields, lit up like a Christmas tree; turrets, battlements, towers, an extravaganza of a house. All thoughts of Sam left my head.

'Holy sweet Jesus!'

He laughed. 'You can't beat the Scots for castles. We've always had great imaginations.'

'Is it haunted?'

'Of course . . . but they have promised me they won't put you in a haunted room. It's one of the jokes they play on visitors.'

'They?'

'Brothers and sisters. They think it's hilarious. Mother goes mad keeping an eye on them whenever there are visitors coming.'

'I don't want to sleep in a haunted room. I'd rather turn round and go home.'

'I promise, a huge solemn oath. Your stay will be ghostless.'

He drew to a stop at the foot of high granite steps and the door was thrown open and out flooded children, dogs, light and shadow, noise, laughter and the yapping of a small excited dog. Merriment was the word that came into my head, great merriment flooding out from the house and embracing us. The door of the car was opened and a hand appeared and I was pulled out into the crowd.

'Welcome, a most hearty welcome to our un-English guest. Yippee.' A young man in a kilt whirled me round.

'Help, help,' I cried as I whirled, like a mad dream, round and round amongst the laughter and the yapping dogs. 'Marcus, help me.'

He caught me just inside the hall door and held me tight against himself and with one fist gently boxed the ears of the kilted man. 'Manners, Angus. She is a poor tired traveller. Polly, everyone, this is Polly, please be gentle with her. She doesn't have a bumptious family like ours. Mother, Mother, come and pacify your brood. Polly, this is Angus; he is tertius. I am secundus, only a year between us. Andrew is primus ... you will be saved from meeting him, as he is seeing in the New Year in Australia. He is learning about large-scale sheep farming, so that he can run this place and make our fortune.'

The words whirled in my head as the children danced around me, and I was sure that if Marcus had not been there to hold on to me I would have fallen down in some kind of stupor. Silence fell suddenly as a door at the back of the hall opened and a tall grey-haired woman came through it. The dogs left off their yipping and playing and rushed to surround her. She walked straight across the hall to me, her hand outstretched.

'Welcome, Polly. Forgive my unruly children. I hope your journey wasn't too exhausting. These, I do have to say, are not all my bairns; this is where the cousins all come to celebrate the New Year. We have a very full house.' As she spoke she put her arm through mine and we walked across the hall, followed by Marcus. 'And how is your brother Sam?' she asked.

I wondered whether to correct her or not. What would Grandma say?

'Actually he's my uncle.'

'Forsooth,' she said.

There was a little snort of laughter from Marcus, behind me.

'My father was his oldest brother. Greg. He was killed in the war.' There was silence; maybe, I thought, she didn't approve of the war, like Grandpa, and then I remembered about Marcus's father.

'I thought Ireland was neutral.'

'It was, but quite a lot of—'

'Yes, yes,' she said, quite brusquely. 'Of course.' She stopped walking; we had arrived at the bottom of a majestic flight of stairs, which curled upwards towards a dark landing. The thought of ghosts prickled my skin.

'Catholic?'

The word shot from her mouth. Like a bullet from a gun.

'No. I'm . . . we're . . .'

'I see. Marcus, show Polly to her room. I hope you will be comfortable, my dear.'

She swept off into the darkness of a long passage, her feet clicking on the flagstone floor. He touched my shoulder and gave me a small nudge towards the stairs. I started to climb, his steps behind me heavy on the Turkey carpet.

'Did I upset her?'

'Mother? Heavens no. She's a bit obscure from time to time. She lives in a dimension of her own. We all love her to bits but we don't pay much attention to her. She really mistrusts Catholics, so at least you gave her the right answer there. Turn right at the top. Hogmanay has been in her charge ever since my father was killed. She takes it very seriously. It's more importamt to her than Christmas. Here we are.'

He pushed open a door on the left and I followed him into an enormous room. A fire flickered in the grate and the furniture, large and sombre, seemed to tremble in the light of the flames.

'Crumbs! Golly!'

'Guaranteed ghostless.'

There was wild wallpaper on the walls, huge pink ramping flowers, climbing up to the darkness of the ceiling.

'I bet even your queen doesn't have a room this size.'

'She probably does in Scotland. I'll leave you to tidy up and come back in about half an hour. I wouldn't want you to get lost trying to find your way downstairs.' He touched my shoulder and then was gone and the door shut behind him with a strange deep thud. I hoped he had been telling the truth about the ghosts.

Later that evening, after we had eaten and sung songs round the piano in the great hall, and had played charades and generally overheated ourselves, I set off up the stairs, hoping that I would be able to find my bedroom. There was the sound of footsteps running up the stairs behind me and Marcus put his hand on my shoulder.

'Shh,' he said low in my ear. 'Don't say a word.' He guided me across the landing and along the passage, and put out his hand to open the door.

'No. You're not coming in.'

'Shh,' he repeated, and opened the door. He gave me a gentle shove and then I heard the door close behind me. The light on the table beside the bed was on, making a pool of brightness, but the rest of the room was shadowy and flickering, lit only by the fire; the flames leapt high up into the chimney and a tall thin man was standing by the fireplace. He lifted his arms and held them out towards me.

'Baby.'

I swear that my heart stopped for a moment and then I ran across the huge floor space between us and he caught me in his arms and held me tight.

'Sam.'

He kissed my neck and my face and my hair and then put me down on the ground and stared at me, up and down. He held my hands tight so that I couldn't move away. Up and down his eyes moved slowly. I was dizzy and breathless and my heart was jumping inside me, and his eyes continued with their voyaging and neither of us spoke. A piece of wood fell from the fire, breaking the silence, and then we both spoke absurdly at once.

'You gave me such a fright.'

'Darling Baby, I thought . . .'

He let go of my hands and I stepped backwards, away from him.

'Don't go!'

I laughed. 'How can I go? Where can I go?'

He caught my hand again and pulled me towards the armchair by the fire; he sat down and pulled me on to his knee.

'So he never told you?'

'Who? Marcus? No, not a word. Do his parents know you're here?'

'Heavens no. No one knows, only Marcus and you.'

'But why? Why, Sam, all this nonsense?' I began to pound his chest with my fist. 'Why, why, why have you not been in touch with Grandpa and Grandma? Sam, I don't want to cry. I really don't want to cry.'

'Then don't cry, silly Baby. Stop punching me, calm down and I'll tell you everything. Oh, God, Baby, it's so good to see you. You have no idea how lonely I've been for you.' He plunged his face down into my hair and we sat in silence once more. I didn't cry.

After a while, quite a long while, he raised his head and adjusted his position in the chair, pushing me well down beside him, one of his arms around my shoulders.

'I know you're cross with me, but there is nothing I can do. I can apologise, say sorry, forgive me, but I don't suppose that will have much effect. Do you know, I have loved you since the day you were born. More even than Jassie. Differently from the way I loved Jassie. You were mine. Nonie said we could share you and then she went away and so you became mine. Then she married Charlie and had those other two and you became even more mine. Do you remember that picnic we went on, with Marcus, in Maher's boat? Remember that?' I nodded. 'Good. I'm glad. That was a day to remember. That was the day ...'

'Marcus talked about Klimt. I'd never heard the name before. I remember that day. Now I have three Klimt reproductions in my room. He was right about the gold, you know. I do remember that day. The cow bellowed and the water was so warm and—'

'And I fell in love with you.'

'I was only twelve, for heaven's sake.'

'That doesn't matter.'

'Of course it matters.'

'Well you're not twelve now.'

'No.'

'I can love you with impunity.'

I giggled. 'What's that?'

'You must look it up in the dictionary when you get home. Laugh, Baby, laugh. I love it when you laugh that great big laugh of yours. I know you're angry with me, darling. I know you think I have behaved in the most hideous way—'

'You have.'

'— but I think it's for the best. It's better that Father thinks I'm off sowing wild oats, something like that that he can understand. He'll never understand about the Cubans and what they're trying to do, not in a million years. He'll never understand. He will believe that I've joined the enemy, that I've sold my soul to the devil. And poor Mama will be so sad for him and she will half believe his rantings and be sad for me too. Better that they're both angry. Anger keeps you marching along, it really does.'

'They're too old to march. You're just afraid of Grandpa. You don't want him to shout at you. You don't want him to do his domestic tyrant bit. You're just running away. You are afraid to tell him what you're up to. I never thought you were afraid of anything.'

Then I felt stupid and became silent. A few silly words knocked in my head. *Afraid. Never thought. Afraid. Never. Anything. Anything at all. Never. Sam. Afraid.* He was talking and I couldn't hear him; I could only hear my own words. *Afraid. Running. Sam. Samsamsam.*

Growling words, screeching words; soon my head would burst.

He shook my shoulder. 'Would you listen to me.'

'Ow, you're hurting me. You always hurt me. That's how you win arguments. Hurt.'

He let go of my arm. 'Polly. Polly.'

'What?' Disgruntled voice. This was not the way I had wanted things to be. The happiness that I had been filled with when I saw him first had leached away.

'Do you hate me?'

I didn't answer.

'You have to tell me, Baby, because if you hate me,

really hate me, I will go. Now.' He took his hands from me and held them up above his head, as if he were in front of a firing squad.

'Of course I don't hate you. I'm just annoyed with you.'

His hands came slowly down; the fire hissed and spat and I thought of Grandpa and Paddy Deery's wood. 'That wood is damp.'

'That's not our problem, thank God. Come here to me, Baby. Kiss me and then tell me why you're cross with me.' He put his arms round me again and pulled me close and kissed my mouth with such sweetness that I almost fainted.

'If that's what impunity means, I like it.'

'Not angry? Promise.'

'Of course I'm angry.'

'Just one more kiss and then we'll talk.'

'Sam . . .'

'Ssssshh.'

Hours later, or anyway a long time as the fire had burnt down to a red pit of ash, he struggled to his feet and held out a hand towards me. 'Up.'

'I can't move.'

'Up, Baby. Come on, it's way past your bedtime.'

'I'm not going to bed. You haven't talked to me yet.'

'I'm going to build up the fire again and you're going to get into bed and then I will sit beside you and talk.'

'Bedtime stories.'

'If that's what you want.'

'You know what I want.'

I took his hand and he pulled me to my feet. I felt like a wreck. It had been a long way from Dublin to this place, wherever it might be, and a long way from being a child to being a grown-up girl. I was exhausted by the effort of it all. He busied himself with the logs by the fireplace and I found my nightdress wrapped round a hot water bottle. I checked to make sure that his back was turned and threw off my clothes; I pulled the warm nightdress over my head and jumped into bed. The sheets were cold, smooth and cold as ice, but there were three bottles, one just below my pillow, one halfway down and the third making a wonderful warm hollow for my feet. The ceiling was high and dark and filled with creeping shadows; I was glad he was there in the room with me.

'You're not to fall asleep on me. Hear me, Baby. No sleeping. In fact I'm coming in beside you. You can lend me one of those bottles. God almighty but it's chilly.' He sat on the edge of the bed and took off his shoes and socks and then slid in beside me. 'I need you to keep me warm. Here, give me one of those bottles for my feet and then tell me about the dear old people. It's no wonder the Scots have bright red faces and wear kilts: this must be the coldest country in the world. Now, that's better. Speak, my lady, speak.'

Warm, together, I wondered where to begin. In my mind it had been so easy. I was going to give him a good dressing down, in Grandpa's words, but here and now, wrapped in his arms, I couldn't.

'He is not a domestic tyrant, you know that. We all know that. Grandma says he's not and she should know. He's getting so old and I'm sure he's ill; he hasn't been well since Pluto died. Old, crabbed, sitting upstairs in his library all alone and then he had a row with the Whelans. And Harry's raging with him because he isn't engaged to Katie any longer and Grandma's upset about everything and then you go and disappear, and they know I know something and he keeps asking me and I have nothing to say. If you could just send them a postcard. Something. Oh, Sam!'

I stopped talking and stared up at the ceiling. He lay silently and unmoving beside me.

'I am a bastard,' he said finally.

'We all love you so much.' What I didn't dare say was that I loved him so much; I lay there and those words jumped into my mouth and I shut it tight to stop them coming out.

Sam cleared his throat. 'You'll have to explain to me about Harry and the Whelans. Baby?'

'Yes?'

He nuzzled his face into the side of my neck. 'Do you love me, Baby?'

'Everybody loves their uncles.'

'Don't be an ass. That is not what I meant.'

'Anyway, about the Whelans. Harry got engaged to Katie—'

'Boy . . . o! Old Harry got himself engaged. I never thought he'd do that, and to little Miss Whelan, no less. Is she pretty? I only remember her as a kid who used to come to tea from time to time. Are the old dears pleased?'

'If you'd shut up for a minute, I'd tell you.'

'Silent as the grave.'

'Grandma was of course delighted. She likes Dr Whelan and she likes Katie. It all happened the night we had a great thunderstorm and she had us all down in the dining room, candles, shutters closed, the two girls scared out of their wits and Sadie doling out huge slices of cake and cups of tea, and then in comes Harry to tell us he's going to marry Katie and we are all happy and excited and the storm dies down and they send me to bed.' I sighed. 'That's one of the problems of not being quite grown up, you get sent to bed. You miss things; there are so many secrets that you miss.' He was kissing my neck. 'Are you listening to me?'

'I surely am. I listen to you always, Baby. When I'm asleep you talk to me, when I'm walking down an empty road, or sitting in the bus. I listen to—'

'Oh, do shut up. *Ne temere*. Have you heard of *ne temere*?'

'Of course I have, but—'

'Grandpa said that to Harry and Harry went a bit wild and then Grandma sent me to bed and I don't know what they said to each other after I left.'

'You'll make a rotten spy.'

'Well that's the way it was. I had no idea what he was talking about and Nonie just made silly faces when I mentioned it to her. Anyway, it's to do with mixed marriages and swearing before God to bring up the children as Romans and Grandpa said it was a terrible invasion of freedom and he didn't give a damn if his grandchildren wanted to become Romans but they should not be forced to. He fought for freedom he said and so did Harry. And Greg and Jassie . . .'

'Yes,' said Sam. He sat up and rubbed at his face with his hand.

'That was at half term when he said that.'

'Half term?'

'I went down for four days and he really wasn't well and the Whelans asked us to dinner the night before I left and Grandma told him that he was to behave himself and he was great until . . . until the pudding and then he started in about the whole thing and Mrs Whelan got angry and Grandma said we had to leave. It was all quite embarrassing and Harry was raging and he and I had to practically drag Grandpa out to the car and Harry said yes he was a domestic tyrant and everyone was upset and they sent me to bed again the moment we got home. I'm sixteen now, so maybe they won't do that any more.'

'I think they're protecting you, keeping you safe from something that could hurt you.'

'But that's what the Whelans say they're doing . . .'

'The degree is different. They are determining that she has a safe place in heaven, we just don't want you to get too bruised on earth.'

'We? Why do you say we?'

'Because I agree with them. I don't want to see you get too bruised on earth either, but there's not much any of us can do to stop it. We can try a little. Youth's the season made for joy.'

'Grandma said that to me once.'

'She would, it's one of her wisdoms. She likes to believe it's true. Go on with your story.'

'Well, I was going the next day and while we were having our breakfast Harry came in. He looked awful and he started to boss us all around, then he shouted at Grandpa and threw the ring at him and Grandpa got upset and left the room and it was grim.'

'Katie had given him back the ring?'

'It was Grandpa's mother's ring. Katie didn't actually give it back to him, her mother did.'

He made a mournful whistling noise. 'Poor old Harry. Poor old sod.'

'Everyone cried and then Mr Riordan came for me and I had to go. I always have to go. It isn't fair.'

'Well that's a baby remark if ever I heard one.'

'Yes, I suppose it is. The thing is, Grandma rang me on Christmas Day and she sounded awful and all she wanted to know was if I'd heard from you. So you see.'

'See what?'

'You know perfectly well what I mean. You're not being helpful, not at all. You must let them know that you're all right. You must let them know something.'

'I'm grown up. I can walk around the world without telling my parents where I'm going. I don't have to ask permission any longer. You'll know what I mean soon. Any moment. I don't want to hurt them, Baby, I just want to live my own life. Now. Not wait until they're dead. You have to break away.'

He turned away from me and sat up, swinging his legs over the side of the bed, down on to the floor. Past the blackness of his body I could see the full moon through the window, like a huge half-crown piece hanging against the mass of flinty stars, not a cloud to be seen.

'Well, I'm sick of telling lies for you. Why didn't you leave me in the dark too?'

He shook his head. 'I . . . I couldn't.'

That seemed to be all that he was going to say. There was a long silence.

'You have to break away,' he repeated. 'From all those loveable enfolding things that hold you so tight. They stop you from looking at the reality of the world, the cruelty, the injustice, the blackness of injustice. When you leave that warmth you just long to be back, cuddling down.' He began to laugh. 'What a bloody fool I sound. A king of fools. I remember the day you were born. Everyone made such a fuss and I was raging. You had stolen my thunder and then they took me in to see you and the moment I looked at you, little pink squirmy thing, the smallest human being that I had ever seen, I knew that I would love you for ever. So you see, I had to tell you something. I couldn't go away without seeing you. Am I not, darling Baby, a king of fools?'

'Yes,' I said.

Of course he had told me nothing and it was not until I woke the next morning that I realised what a fool I had been to have paid attention to his love talk. It was still dark when I woke, but with no moon outside the big grey windows; the fire was crackling merrily, so he must have seen to it before he left. On the pillow beside my head he had left a letter and with it in the envelope the signet ring that he had always worn on the little finger of his left hand. It was a dark carnelian carved with the head of some mythological animal with its hair blowing in some ancient and equally mythological wind and one claw raised in either anger or salute, all sunk in a thick gold setting. All the boys had rings like this, but Sam was the only one who had worn his all the time. I still wear it on the fourth finger of my right hand.

Dearest Baby,

You look so peaceful sleeping all curled up into your pillows and blankets. I love every bit of you, but I seem to have said that a thousand times last night and you will be bored with those words if you have to hear them again. What

I have to say though is what I avoided saying last night and that is that I am off now, in the next few days. I cannot tell you where, but I hope to be able to write to you and let you know how I am. Please, please don't tell the old people that you have seen me, or know anything of my movements. I do not want to cause them more pain than I already have. One day I will come back for you and maybe you will be persuaded to come with me. I give you my ring. Maybe, of course, your life will have taken you in some other direction, but that is a punishment I will have to face.

Ever yours. Uncle and lover.

I read it twice. I was filled with rage and sorrow. I read it again and then tore it into shreds and walked over to the fireplace and sprinkled the tiny pieces of paper into the flames. I contemplated throwing the ring after them, but the thought of burning the family's crest suddenly horrified me so I pushed it deep down into my sponge bag instead.

The subject of Sam was not mentioned until I was saying goodbye to Marcus at the airport the day after all the fun and jollification. He had just kissed me on the cheek and was holding me by the elbow.

'So?'

It was a question. I felt my face getting red. 'It was a lovely party. I really enjoyed myself. Thank you so much for inviting me.'

'Don't be an ass, Polly. You know what I mean.'

'Where is he? Where has he gone?'

'I honestly don't know. He just appeared and disappeared. We had no conversation.'

'You must have known he was coming.'

'Well . . . yes.'

'You set me up.'

'No harm meant, dear girl. Really no harm. It was just a bit of enjoyable fun. A Hogmanay surprise. Don't be cross with me.'

'Promise me that if he gets in touch again you'll let me know.'

'I can't do that. Honestly no, Poll. He's my friend. I can't betray him like that. Let's take this as a bit of fun and leave it at that.'

'You may think it's fun but he's really upsetting Grandma and Grandpa. That's not funny. My father was killed in the war and Jassie and now he goes and disappears on them.' I was shouting. I pulled my elbow from his grip and dashed off along the passage towards the plane. 'Lovely party. Thanks,' I shouted back at him as I ran. Bloody, I said to myself inside my head, bloody, bloody.

Nonie met me at the airport. It was cold, sleet falling from a dark grey sky as she tucked my arm through hers.

'We've missed you.'

'I was only away for two days.'

'Just the same. Did you have a good time? Did they love your dress? You look wrecked. I bet you never went to bed.'

'Of course I went to bed. Yes, I had a great time. Marvellous. I don't think anyone noticed my dress; they all wore kilts and scarves and rugs and sashes and long plaid skirts and daggers in their socks and silver buttons and velvet jackets and they drank the health of the Old Pretender and the Young Pretender and they all said they loved me because I wasn't English and nobody noticed my dress and everyone drank the most enormous amount and there were bagpipes and my feet are agony.'

'Golly,' said Nonie. 'I hope no one raped you.'

'Don't be silly, the Scots don't do things like that.'

'Don't be too sure.' She unlocked the door of the car. 'Hop in. Quick, or we might freeze to death. You must think up great stories to tell the children, not just sore feet stories, but stories about young Lochinvar and Bonnie Prince Charlie, and ghoulies and ghosties, real Scottish tales.'

I thought of my story, the story without beginning or end that I couldn't tell anyone, and almost blurted it out there and then to Nonie, but I knew she would insist that I told Grandma, that it was best that she should know what her youngest son was up to.

No.

No, no, no.

The day was almost gone. The wind slashed the sleet against the windscreen; at the bus stops people huddled under their umbrellas and looked dispirited. It didn't look like a happy new year, more like a very exhausted old one.

*　　*　　*

Grandpa became very ill.

Looking back from where I am now, so many years

later, I can still hardly bear to write those four words.

Grandma and Nonie conspired with each other not to say a word about it to me; I'm sure that Charlie had a hand in this secrecy also. All, of course, in my best interests: Polly must not be upset, death is for grown-ups to know and whisper about; death happens and then we all wipe away our tears and pass on to the rest of our lives; the young have not got the capacity, the wisdom, to do this, so we must keep it from them. Death is one thing, dying another: anger, pain and fear, even sometimes madness, dementia; the children must be protected. Polly must at all costs be protected.

But Harry didn't think so.

February has always been the one month that I really hate, still do; nothing good ever happens then, the sun doesn't shine and the world seems grey and full of diseases. One afternoon in late February I was standing just outside the gates of my school talking to a friend. What were we talking about? That I don't remember, it's too long ago; I do remember though that I was attaching my satchel to the carrier on the back of my bike when a car drove up beside me and a voice called my name. It sounded like Harry's voice. I bent and peered in the open window of the car. It was Harry all right.

'Harry! What—'

'Hop in.'

'I can't. I have my bike.'

'Don't argue. Your friend will take your bike. Won't you, love? Quick, Poll, don't dawdle. We have a long way to go.'

'Nonie—'

'It's OK. Get in.' He leant across and opened the door. He smiled at my friend. 'It's so good of you. I'm not kidnapping her, I promise you.'

I let go of the bike and she took it, and I got into the car. He gave me the breath of a kiss on the cheek and drove off into the traffic.

'My homework—'

'Homework be damned.'

I waved at my friend, standing somewhat stupefied on the pavement; she raised her hand and we were round the corner.

'I have spoken to Nonie.'

'What's all this about, Harry? Are we eloping or something? I don't think I want to elope with you.'

'Don't be an ass. It's about him. I think he's dying, Poll. Honest to God. And he keeps asking for you . . . well, Jassie. I will go with Jassie, he cries. He wakes up and calls Jassie, Jassie, come and get me. Poor Mama is in an awful state and Sadie keeps making him soup, which he won't drink. Dr Whelan wants him to go into hospital and he adamantly refuses to go. So you see?'

'No, I don't see. Why has no one told me? I've spoken to Grandma on the phone and she said everyone was all right. She said that Grandpa was thinking about getting another dog. She said . . . she . . . she didn't say anything about him . . . dying. Oh, Harry!' Tears poured out of my eyes and rolled down my cheeks.

'Cry all you want, but finish up with the tears before you get there. Tears they don't need. So bawl your head off now. Here.' He handed me a large clean handkerchief. I covered my face with it and sobbed. He talked on and on and I didn't hear a word. I just felt the sway of the car and heard Grandpa's voice saying I will go with Jassie, I will go with Jassie, I will go . . . The tears had stopped. I blotted at my face and then scrumpled up the sodden handkerchief. Harry had stopped talking.

He looked wretched. I wondered if he and Katie had got back together again.

'Um . . .' I said. I opened the window and quickly threw out the sodden mass of handkerchief before shutting the window again.

'Hey,' he said. 'That's mine.'

'It was disgusting. You wouldn't have wanted it again. When I'm rich I'll buy you a whole box. Linen, with your initials hand-stitched in the corner.'

'Thanks a whole lot. I will look forward to that.'

'Have you and Katie made it up?'

There was a very long pause. I thought that he was not going to answer my question.

'No.'

We drove for a mile or so in silence and I wished that I had kept my mouth shut.

'It's her bloody mother. She has made her promise not to see me again.'

'She can't do that.'

'She's done it. I went down to see Katie. I thought we should talk the whole thing through, come to some sort of compromise. That should be possible, wouldn't you have thought? Mrs Whelan answered the door and marched me into the sitting room. I felt as if I were about twelve and being carpeted by the head: serious stuff. She said that the bishop had said that people like her had to set an example to everyone else, people with education and a position in the community should lead by example. Otherwise the Church would be weakened, the faithful would drain away, souls would be lost. I wanted to laugh and then I got so angry. Pa is right, I thought, and then I pulled myself together and said that I wanted to see Katie. I honestly did not think that she would go down that road after her mother.'

'But she did?'

He nodded. 'She did indeed.'

There was another long pause.

'She looked so young and pathetic when she came into the room . . . so . . . so loveable and I loved her so much. I haven't spoken about this to anyone, so it is hideously raw in my throat. Her mother left the room and called upstairs to her and she came running down the stairs. I knew by the sound of her running feet that she thought I was going to give in, I knew by the smile she gave me when she ran through the door. I could not smile at her; I just stood there by the window like a fucking eejit. She stopped smiling.

– Hello, Harry.

– We have to talk. Alone, Katie. Will you come for a walk?

She glanced towards her mother.

– Or a drive?

– We can talk here. Why don't you sit down?

– I can't. I'd rather stand.

We stood. Mrs Whelan looked at her feet, I looked at Katie and her eyes fluttered round and round the room, not lighting on anyone or anything.

– Katie darling . . .

– Do you love me?

– Darling, you know I love you. I'm crazy about you.

– Then . . .

I held out my hand towards her. Come for a walk.

She glanced again at her mother. Mrs Whelan shook her head. We were going to get nowhere.

– Look, Harry, you don't have to become a Catholic, you really don't. Mammy has agreed to that. She says it is all right with the bishop, but you must agree to sign . . .

— I want to talk to you alone. If not now, later today. Tomorrow. Soon, for God's sake.

She shook her head.

— Why not?

— I have promised Mammy.

— What? What have you promised her?

Her voice was so low that I had to step closer to her to hear her words.

— Not to see you again until you agree.

— Katie! Do you think that God — your God — will be pleased with you? Do you really think that he wishes us both to be so unhappy? Hey? Do you honestly think that he, whoever he is, wherever he may be, thinks there is a difference between a child that has a cross on its forehead and one that has not? Water splashed on it? Surely he embraces all children, black, white, Christian, heathen? Aren't you taught that in Sunday school or wherever it is you learn about such stuff? I wouldn't want any child of mine taught that dangerous rubbish. Pretty unchristian too when you come to think about it.

I looked over at Mrs Whelan and saw that she was staring at me with eyes of terrible malevolence.

– I suppose I should go . . .

– We wouldn't want to keep you.

– Darling Katie, you don't have to make stupid promises to your mother or to any bishop who may ask you. When you realise that, I'll be waiting, I promise.'

He wearily pulled a hand across his forehead. 'End of story,' he said.

'Oh, Harry!'

'Don't for God's sake cry any more.'

'I'm not going to.'

'I haven't got another handkerchief.' He laughed at his own rotten joke.

'Why did you promise her that?'

'I had set so much store by her, by the very thought of marrying her. It was something I never thought would happen to me. In fact I didn't believe in the existence of the thing they all call love. It never occurred to me that the time would come when I and my own family would take over Kildarragh. That we would carry on that wonderful slog, keeping the place afloat, another generation, working and playing and building. I thought it would go on another while. It's not a bad tradition, is it? What do you think?'

I shook my head.

'I'm forty-one,' he said. His voice sounded full of despair. I put out my hand and touched the side of his face; it was hot and scratchy, as if he hadn't shaved for several days.

'It will all come out OK. You'll see. Don't fret, dear Harry.'

There was another very long silence.

'I will sit beside him and hold his hand. If he calls me Jassie I won't argue. Oh, Harry, what's it going to be like?'

'Everyone dies,' was all he said.

We arrived in the rain and the house looked small and dark by the standards of Marcus's house. The two lamps by the hall door trembled in the wind.

'Four hours,' he said as he stopped the car at the door. 'We'll just be in time for dinner.' He gave my shoulder a squeeze. 'Be cheery.'

The hall door was thrown open and Grandma was standing there, her arms spread wide.

'Nonie rang,' she shouted, and the wind tossed the words out into the darkness. 'Come quick, my darlings, out of the cold. Nonie rang. So I am no longer surprised.'

I jumped out of the car and ran into her waiting arms. She held me tight and spoke and the words, bullied by the wind, rose over my head and away towards the ocean. 'I was surprised, I do have to say, when she rang and told me that you had been kidnapped by bad Harry.' We were in the warmth of the hall and Harry had come in behind us and slammed the door. She looked tired and old, her faced lined as I had never seen it before. 'Bad Harry,' she repeated. He laughed and then she laughed and I just felt happy to be home.

'You'd have said no if I'd told you what I was going to do,' said Harry.

'Perhaps. But come along now, the lovely pair of you. Wash your hands and come and sit to dinner.'

'Grandpa . . .'

'After you've eaten. He'll have eaten too. There's a nurse there at the moment shovelling food into him and he resists that. He'll be so pleased to see you.'

'A nurse?'

'He needs a nurse,' said Harry. 'It's too much for Mother to cope with. Dr Whelan found us a nice woman.'

'Ah.'

I followed them both into the dining room, then I remembered that I hadn't washed my hands and turned and dashed out of the door, colliding with Sadie crossing the hall.

'Trying to kill me, Baby dear?' she gasped, then grasping me with both her hands she pulled me to her. 'You're a sight for sore eyes, Baby dear. Cheer them up, there's a girl, that's what they need. Where are you flying off to anyway?'

'I have to wash my hands.'

'Run then. Scoot. You don't want the soup to get cold.'

Be cheery, be cheery, cheer them up.

The water ran warm over my hands and whispered the words at me; I scrubbed at my face also and rinsed it and felt marginally comforted by the feel of the warm water on my skin. I went back into the dining room with a big smile cracking across my face.

'There you are,' said Grandma, 'looking nice and pink. Now I want to hear all about Marcus's castle.'

So I told them, driven by desperation to keep cheery, a splendid Highland tale of kilts and castles and bagpipes and whisky and reels and tartans and everything under the sun except for the one thing that they really would have liked to know and I really would have liked to have been able to tell them.

✻   ✻   ✻

You always had to push his bedroom door hard to get it to move across the carpet enough for you to squeeze in; the slight scraping noise this made must have wakened him, because he was lying with his eyes open staring at the door. His eyes were sunk deep down into what flesh there was stretched over his face. His hair stood in a spiky halo round his head; his hands lay on the covers, larger than I had ever seen them before.

Large hands, long, long fingers, like snakes they seemed.

'Someone is there.' His voice was barely audible.

The nurse got up from her chair near the fire and came towards me, smiling.

'You must be Polly.'

I nodded, afraid to speak, afraid that my voice might sound like thunder in his frail ears.

She gestured towards his bed. 'He will be so pleased to see you. I'll pop down to the kitchen and have a cup of tea, and leave the pair of you in peace.' She crossed the room silently and was gone out of the door. I moved towards the bed and stood by him looking down and wondering whether to take his hand or touch his face or kiss him or . . . He opened his eyes and stared up at me.

'Jassie,' he said, and his voice was surprisingly clear. 'My dear girl, I have waited for you for so long.'

I wanted to argue, but I didn't: I sat down on the edge of his bed and put my hand on his. He seemed to smile.

'Darling,' I said.

His fingers moved under mine. 'Shh. Let's just sit here,' he whispered. 'Just sit.'

So I sat there beside him and he seemed to drift into a sleep and the fire made its friendly noises and I imagined I could hear the sniffling and the occasional thump of Pluto's tail as he guarded his old man. Those imaginary sounds gave me comfort. After what seemed like a long time the door opened and after a moment Grandma laid her hand on my shoulder.

'Bed, dear child. Tomorrow you shall sit here as long as you wish.'

He opened his eyes; they were quite bright. 'You see, Beatrice? It's Polly. She has been here holding my hand. Isn't it good of her to come?'

'Good night, Grandpa. I'll see you in the morning.'

'I never got round to getting you that pony. When the spring comes, though, when the spring comes. I'll be up and about when the spring comes.'

I bent down and kissed him; his forehead was dry and very cold. I left the room and waited out on the landing for Grandma. She followed me quite quickly and put her arm around my shoulders as we walked along the passage to my bedroom. When we reached the door she kissed me.

'Poor old man,' she sighed, and melted into the dark.

It was still dark when I was awakened by a lone bird whistling; it was a long melodic sound like nothing I had ever heard before. After what seemed like a minute, the whistling stopped and the night became silent once more. I waited hopefully for the bird to sing again, but there was only the occasional sigh from the distant sea. I slept again and only woke when I heard the tap tap of one of the girls sweeping along the passage outside my door. Always the same, tap tap, tap tap, tap tap, round the corner and then the diminishing sound of the brush and the girl's feet pattering lightly down the stairs. Always the same. Always had been the same.

I heard doors opening, closing, the rattle in the drawing room, below my bedroom, of the curtains being opened and the sound of the ashes being raked from the fireplace. All those sounds I loved, that I missed so much when I was in Dublin.

Then somewhere a door banged and I heard Harry's voice. What was he doing here so early in the morning, I wondered. And the squeaking footsteps of the nurse, and voices. Hurried voices, hushed but urgent, and I knew what had happened. He had gone with the singing bird, across the cold grass, over the sand and the sea, to America perhaps, because I knew he didn't believe in heaven, so maybe he had gone to start again in America. The land of the free where he could have central heating and ride a bronco, with Pluto running behind him. I got up and put on my dressing gown and went out on to the landing. I peered over the banisters and saw Grandma folded in Harry's arms and Sadie standing by them both, her face covered by a large handkerchief, her whole body shaking. I ran down the stairs and Grandma pulled herself free of Harry's embrace and caught me on the bottom stair. She kissed me and patted my hair back from my face.

'Darling Baby. He's gone. He waited for you and then he went.'

'Or Jassie.'

'Or Jassie. But you came and made him happy.'

'I heard the bird singing.' I started to cry and we all stood wet-faced in a tight little circle in the hall, Sadie snuffling like some sorrowful beast, the three of us letting our eyes stream in silence.

'I must go and ring the boys,' said Harry, 'and Dr Whelan. And . . .' They all, even Sadie, turned and stared at me.

'I don't know where he is. I promise. I really don't. If I did I'd tell you.'

'We know. We know,' Grandma soothed me. 'Do that, dear Harry, and Sadie will put some breakfast on the table for us. Eating is a good thing to do, an essential thing to do. You can cry into the bacon and eggs, Sadie; your tears will flavour them well.'

Sadie sniffed, snuffled and wiped at her eyes with the

corner of her apron. She threw her head back and roared, 'Holy Mary Mother of God, pray for us sinners now and at the hour of our death.'

'Amen,' said Grandma, and walked me towards the dining room.

'Can I . . . can I . . .'

She pushed me down into my chair. 'When you've had your breakfast. The nurse is tidying the old dear up. We wouldn't want him to look unkempt, would we?'

I started to cry again.

'And we must telephone to Nonie and of course the rector. Oh dear, how the poor old man would hate all that God stuff that has to go on. Have some orange juice, darling.' She picked up a jug and poured some into a glass for me and then some for herself. We could hear Harry's voice clearly through the door.

'Don't worry. Just come. We'll be expecting you for dinner. Yeah yeah, bro. See you.'

A moment later he came back into the room.

'They'll be here by sixish. They're going to ring Nonie and see if she wants a lift down with them or whether she would rather come on her own. Dr Whelan will be here in about half an hour. There's the most marvellous smell of bacon coming up from the kitchen. Isn't it amazing how life just goes doggedly on?'

Grandma laughed. 'Only if you have Sadie in the kitchen.' She sat down and put her head in her hands. 'Such silly little jokes we make. You know, I've cried for him for weeks now. I've gone to bed each night and cried. I knew this would happen. I'm so glad, Baby dear, that you came in time for him to see you . . . maybe he would have waited on and on, who knows, but he saw you. He knew you. Then he could go. It's just so sad about Sam.'

'I could ring Marcus. He might know how to get in touch. He might not. I could try that.'

'Yes.' Her voice sounded very small. 'Yes. You could do that.'

The door opened and one of the girls came in carrying a large tray. Her face was red with crying and her ginger hair stood up on end; I had never seen her before. She put the tray down on the sideboard.

'Yes, Peg. That's very good of you. This is my granddaughter, I don't believe you've met her. Polly, this is Peg. She came to us just before Christmas.'

We nodded at one another and Peg handed round the plates.

'I'll have to come and live here with you, Mother,' said Harry. 'I can never manage to make breakfast for myself. I just have a piece of toast and a cup of tea.'

'We'd probably quite like that, wouldn't we, Peg? And pour out the tea, there's a girl, save my poor old bones getting up and down. Tuck in, dears, don't let it get cold. Yes, and Peg, would you bring another cup for Dr Whelan? I'm sure he'd like a cup of tea when he arrives.'

He arrived just as we were finishing breakfast. He turned the big brass knob on the door and walked with confidence across the hall and into the dining room.

'Dear Mrs Mahony, I am so sorry. I came as fast as I could. So very sorry.' He took her hand and held it for a moment or two. 'Bernadette sends her condolences . . . and . . . um . . . Katie. I tried to persuade her to come, but she was going to Dublin, so . . .'

'Will you have a cup of tea, doctor? Polly will pour you one.'

'No thanks. I'm just after my breakfast. No, I'll just run upstairs . . .'

'A moment, doctor. Polly darling, you must go up and have a few minutes with Grandpa. Then Dr Whelan can do what he has to do, and then you must get dressed, chicken, there will be people coming.'

I got up to go.

'And of course you will ring Marcus. You will try . . .'

'Yes. Of course.'

I approached Grandpa's door with caution; my hand was shaking as I turned the doorknob. A gentle voice spoke, making my heart beat loudly for a moment until I remembered the nurse.

'Come in. I have finished.'

I pushed open the door and went in. The sun streamed into the room, which didn't look at all like my notion of a place of death. A candle flickered in the sunlight on the table by his bed and the table by the window was loaded with flowers. I didn't look at him.

'Thank you,' I said to the nurse. She held out her hand to me.

'It's all right. You're only young. Death shouldn't be frightening. It's a relief from suffering. Look at it that way. Give me your hand.'

I held her hand and she led me towards the bed and

I stood there and gazed at Grandpa while she kept talking. His eyes were closed; I was glad of that. I hadn't been looking forward to having to stare into his unseeing eyes, eyes full of nothing, no laughter, anger, pain, love, just nothing. She held my hand and I considered the old man. His silver hair was brushed across his forehead and his face was white; he did look peaceful, more so than he had last night, I thought. I put out my hand and touched one of his and was startled by how cold it was.

'Some people,' she was saying, 'prefer a darkened room, but I thought with the sun shining and all that he would like that. Mind you, the doctor will be here soon and he may have other thoughts on the subject. What do you think your granny will say?'

'I think he looks great. That will please her.' I wondered why I wasn't crying and then heard his voice in my head: 'Weep no sad tears for me.' I will miss you, Grandpa, but I'm not crying any more. Weep no sad tears for me. I turned away from the old man and smiled at the nurse. 'Thank you. I must now go and get dressed. There will be people coming.'

I backed away from the bed, looking all the time at his white hands, loosely laid on the bedcover.

What would I do without him?

What would we all do without him?

I stretched out my hand behind me and found the knob, cold as his hand, and turned it.

'Goodbye, darling Grandpa.'

'Goodbye, Jassie.' I heard the words as clear as a bell; as clearly as I had heard the bird whistling its notes last night.

* * *

The rector came and he, Grandma and Harry shut themselves in the drawing room and their voices rose and fell and even little bursts of laughter could be heard through the door.

I managed to get hold of Marcus, mainly by sitting by the telephone in the hall and letting Mrs O'Keefe in the post office do the hard work.

'Did I hear a sad thing, Polly?' was the first question that she asked. 'About the general? A sad thing?'

'Yes, Mrs O'Keefe. I'm afraid——'

'Sad indeed. We'll all miss him. How's your granny bearing up? Is she strong in herself?'

'She's——'

'She has a great strength. Tell her I'll be up in the afternoon. To pay my respects like. And Sadie. What would you do without Sadie at all?'

I finally got her to ring Scotland and I could hear her breathing all the way through my conversation with Marcus. He pleaded ignorance of Sam's whereabouts, and of course I didn't know whether to believe him or not. I finally put down the phone filled with amicable mistrust and went to tell Grandma of my lack of progress.

I didn't go back into Grandpa's room again. I brought visitors to the door, but never passed through it. There was a constant stream throughout the day; the men from the farm, holding their hats under their arms and very conscious of their dirty boots, shuffled their feet, leaving little tracks of mud on the carpet. Their wives came too, not with their men, but carrying small gifts of home-made jam or eggs or a brown loaf fresh from the oven wrapped in a clean tea towel; some came in the kitchen door and some came in the front door, some brought a child by the hand, some left their children in the back yard. The parish priest came and was ushered into the drawing room by Sadie herself and served with coffee from the silver pot; as the afternoon wore on the shopkeepers arrived, up the front steps, the postman, and the black-hatted undertaker and his men. Grandma looked dignified but as the day wore on very tired. Nonie telephoned and she and Grandma whispered to each other for what seemed like hours before Grandma handed the receiver to me.

'Darling.'

'Nonie.'

We both spoke at the same time. Then we were both silent for a moment or two.

'Beatrice told me.'

'Yes.'

'I'm so sorry. Are you all right?'

'Yes.'

'She says the funeral will be tomorrow.'

'Yes.'

'I will come down early in the morning. I will be with you by half past nine. Then you can come home with me when it's all over.'

'I want to stay here.'

'No arguments, darling. You have your exams coming up. You must come home. Must, must, must. That's all there is to it. Give Beatrice a big kiss from me. See you tomorrow.' She put down the receiver.

I ran across the hall, through Grandma's winter garden, down the granite steps, across the avenue towards the tennis court, through the oak wood, towards the sea, towards somewhere empty, somewhere there was a fine clean wind.

Down by the sea it was buffeting the spray over the rocks and the bent grass at the back of the beach. The sea did not look appetising, but grey and surly, with angry little ripples of white. It was cold. I shivered and regretted having run from the house without my coat; the spray was cold on my face and stung my eyes, but I was alone. That was what I wanted. Alone. Above me grey birds coasted in a grey sky, and away out to sea I could see the misty shape of the islands.

'Sam.' I yelled my loudest. He must hear me. 'Sam. Come home. Sam. They need you. Sam. Sam.'

I stood on a rock just a few feet above the sea and that was my prayer and one of the birds mewed and came swooping down almost to the level of the water and then soared once more and continued to coast.

'Sam.'

I need you. I whispered those words into myself. My mouth was filled with the taste of the sea as it never could be in Dublin. This was my home. This was where I wanted to be for ever. I heard a sound, the slur of a stone maybe or the crackling of the bracken as someone trod on it, and I turned. Harry was standing just behind me, a large woolly jumper over his arm.

'Here.' He held it out to me. 'What did you go goofing off like that for, without a coat, in your city shoes? Sadie saw you dashing across the avenue and came to fetch me. She said you looked crazy and that you'd catch your death of cold and we don't have time for that now.' He laughed. 'What would we do without Sadie?'

I pulled the jumper over my head; I hadn't realised how perished I was. He put his arms round me and hugged me into his warmth.

'But jokes apart,' I said, 'are we useless people? How will we ever manage without her? Are we incapable of looking after ourselves?'

'Darling Baby, we will have to learn to look after ourselves.'

'Will that be a hard job?' We had started walking slowly back towards the house.

'Probably, but we'll make it in time. You've ruined your shoes.'

'Yes. Now that Grandpa is gone maybe you could sign Katie's bit of paper?'

He shook his head. 'No. I won't do that. He was right, you know. He just went the wrong way about dealing with it.'

'Did you love him?'

'What a daft question to ask. We all loved him.'

'Do you think it matters that he thought I was Jassie?'

'Your head is full of daft questions. Of course it didn't matter. He loved you both; you slipped into her shoes and sometimes, towards the end, he couldn't tell the difference. That was all. It made him happy to think that she was still alive; it made him happy to think that you were here too. Come on, we'll go in the kitchen door, otherwise you will leave wet and slimy trails all over the hall and Sadie will have a fit.'

The kitchen was full of people, from as Sadie would have said every art and part; some I recognised and some I didn't. Hands reached out for Harry and within moments he had disappeared, sucked into the crowd. I slipped out of the door again and ran up the stairs. The house seemed to be filled with whispers, low rumbles of voices sounding through every door, people's soft footsteps on the carpets. I wondered if Marcus had contacted Sam.

Was Sam on his way?

Surely he was on his way.

'Polly!'

Grandma was leaning against the wall outside the drawing room door. She stretched her hand out towards me. I ran across the hall to her.

'I don't want to see anyone else. I want to run away.' She clutched at my hand. I held hard on to her. 'They're here. The men . . . you know. Upstairs with . . . with . . .'

'Yes, darling. I'll get Harry. You can run away with him.'

'No, no. Someone has to hold the fort. I want to run away on my own, just down the garden. I want to be alone for a while. I might go and sit by the tennis court.'

'I'll get you a coat.'

'A coat.' She looked puzzled by the word.

'It's not very nice out.'

'Oh yes, a coat. That would be good of you, dear child.' She let go of my fingers.

The armoire in the cloakroom held coats of all sizes and shapes; I pulled a long black one with a fur collar from its hanger and brought it across the hall to Grandma.

'Thank you, my darling.'

'Will I come with you?'

'No, no, no. I just want to be on my own. Solitude. I want to remember my old tyrant in solitude.' She put on the coat. 'Call Harry. Tell him to hold the fort, till I get back, revived. I will be revived.' She was gone, out through the hall door into her winter garden and down the steps. I went to call Harry.

It was a crawling day. People came and went; the undertaker's men went and came back several hours later with a coffin; I ran upstairs and shut myself into my room. I could hear them bumping up the stairs and across the landing, Harry grey in the face walking slowly behind them. Mickey and Paddy arrived about tea time;

I watched from my window as they slammed the doors of their car and ran up the steps. I hoped that Grandma was back from her solitude. I hoped that Grandpa was still waiting for them on his bed rather than coffined by the lugubrious men.

I sat on my bed and thought of coffins; I thought of my father and Jassie, whom I had barely known, and wondered if their fragmented bodies had been put in coffins. I thought of Pluto. I had never asked anyone what had happened to him, but I suspect they just dug a hole in the ground and laid his old body into it and Grandpa cried an angry tear. The Indians built pyres and set their loved ones on fire on the banks of the holy river Ganges. I'd read about that. I preferred the thought of doing that to burying Grandpa in the local churchyard. I was sure that he would prefer to go up in flames than to moulder in a box for all eternity.

There was a scratching at the door. I stood up. 'Come in.'

It was Sadie. She held out her hand to me.

'Come now, there's a good girl, to your grandma. She's below in the hall. Put your coat on and give your hair a bit of a comb. They're taking the master, the

Lord keep him, to the church. She'll need you by her side.'

Obediently I went to the dressing table and combed my hair and she got my coat from the wardrobe.

'He loved you, so he did.' I put my arms into the coat that she was holding for me. 'He saw little Jassie in you.' She did up the buttons and patted my head. 'Just be beside her. She loves you too. She doesn't need to be standing there on her own.' I nodded. 'Have you a hankie?' I nodded again. 'We'll go down to her so. It's a bitter time for her.' So we marched across the room and along the passage. His bedroom door was open and the nurse stood at the door and watched as the men lifted the coffin and Harry, Mickey and Paddy fidgeted by the window. I ran down the stairs, followed more sedately by Sadie. Grandma stood at the bottom of the stairs, dressed in the long black coat with the fur collar. She didn't say a word, just held out her hand to me, which I took, and we stood in silence, with Sadie just behind her shoulder holding a huge snowy white handkerchief.

Four men slowly carried Grandpa down the stairs, placing their feet with care on each step as they descended, *We mustn't drop the general* stamped on their faces. Behind them the three brothers trod carefully and the nurse remained at the top of the staircase watching the descent.

Grandma's fingers shivered in mine. As the coffin came level with her she stepped forward and put her hand on it for a moment.

'Dear old tyrant, rest in peace.'

Someone, I don't know who, said Amen and behind me Sadie choked into the handkerchief.

We walked across the hall and through the winter garden and stood on the top step watching the men putting the coffin into the hearse. Everything seemed to move in slow motion, the lifting of their arms, the bending and raising of their heads, their feet stepping towards the hearse. The car doors slammed and they were off in slow motion, crunching over the gravel. Harry, Mickey and Paddy walked behind the hearse, followed by the farm men, their hats held respectfully in their hands. The sun nudged the clouds out of the way and shone with fervour on the straggle of men as they walked down the avenue. The car drew up and Grandma and I got into the back and Grandma tried to pull Sadie in too.

'No, mistress dear, haven't we got the dinner to get? You can't have the two lads coming all the way from Dublin and not give them a bite to eat. The girls and I will stay here and see to things.'

So we drove to the church, the tail of the little procession; Grandma never spoke a word, she just sat in silence, straight-backed, holding my fingers with her cold fingers.

Someone was playing the organ and the quiet notes of 'Sheep May Safely Graze' met us as we walked up the path to the church door. Mr Hempenstall, the rector, was waiting for us.

'Dear Beatrice.' He kissed her, and putting his arm around her shoulder he led her up to the front of the church. The music swelled and I remembered that it was one of his favourite pieces.

'I told Sean to put the heating on, so that he wouldn't be cold,' he was saying to her as we sat ourselves down in the pew behind them.

Grandma laughed. 'What a good and thoughtful man you are.' It was good to see her laugh. 'An angel perhaps.'

'In wolf's clothing. Tell me, my memory is fading

with age, when was he last in here?'

She thought for a moment. 'Forty-five ... yes, it must have been then. When we put up the memorial to Greg and Jassie. You must remember that, the stone in the graveyard. He grumbled but he came. I remember he grumbled at you about that too, but he was pleased to see it there. Yes, he was pleased. I think that must have been the last time. He would be furious with me about this. Maybe he will send a thunderbolt.'

'Beatrice dear, I think he'll be smiling.'

The four men came into the church carrying the coffin, the organist stopped playing and we all stood up. The rector moved from beside Grandma to the little wooden stand where the coffin would rest until the next day. Carefully they placed the coffin on the stand and stood for a moment, their heads bowed. Grandma gave herself a little shake and pulled the fur collar closer round her neck.

'Well, that's done. Thank you so much. I am immensely grateful to you all. Come, Polly, it's time to go home. I'm sure the rector will give you boys a lift, if you don't want to walk back.' And she started to walk briskly up the aisle. I scurried after her.

'I couldn't have stayed. Tomorrow will be bad enough, but I couldn't have stayed another minute, my head is so full of memories.' She muttered the words to me as we reached the door. 'Their grief and my grief is so different. I want to go home and sit by the fire. I haven't got him any flowers. Everyone will think that odd, but I know he wouldn't have wanted them. This is all fuss enough. I won't sleep tonight, you know, and where oh where is that bad boy Sam? Where oh where?'

I would have liked to know the answer to that question myself.

'I thought you knew, Polly. I really thought you knew. I didn't tell Geoffrey, but I did think inside myself that you knew.'

I shook my head. She patted my hand.

'I do know now though that you didn't and I apologise for doubting you.' She patted my hand again and I shook my head again.

The hearse had gone and our car was waiting at the gate with Thomas standing by it and the farm men lined up to one side, their hats still in their hands. As we came out of the gate there was a little ragged clapping from them. She walked over to them and taking each man's hand between her own two she spoke to each one in turn.

I got into the car and waited and Thomas stood by the door as a soldier on duty might. She came at last and he took her arm and helped her into the car.

'Thank you, Thomas.' He put a rug over her knees and she smiled at him. 'What a nice young man you are becoming. A credit to your mother.'

He closed the door quietly and got into his seat. It was a short drive and as we got out Grandma spoke to him again.

'What are your plans? For your life? I'm sure you must have plans in your head.'

He went red in the face and didn't speak.

'You must come up and talk to me about your future. In the meantime you can drive me. When I don't feel like driving myself. Have you got a licence.'

He shook his head. 'No, ma'am.'

She laughed. 'I might have known. Wasn't it lucky that I didn't ask you that until we were safely home? Get a licence. If you have any problems tell me and I will see to it. Get one. Tomorrow. And then come and talk to me about your future. Goodbye now, Thomas. Take care of that car on the long and dangerous journey to the back yard and thank you for driving us to the church.'

That night I dreamed that Sam came back. In my dream he arrived just as we were getting into the car to go to the church. On horseback he cantered up the avenue in his most tidy clothes. Grandma stood, amazed, by the car and he scooped her up in front of him and cantered off again, followed by Pluto. 'Sam,' I called out after him. 'Bring her back. This minute. We need her.' And he laughed, a big rollicking roaring laugh that woke me up and it was morning, the grey winter light pushing its way in through the windows and a girl sweeping the stairs, just like any ordinary day.

✳   ✳   ✳

Nonie arrived when we were in the middle of breakfast. The car drew up at the steps and Paddy and Mickey rushed out to greet her. I felt no urge to, so I remained in my chair.

'It's your mother,' said Grandma.

'I don't want to go home with her. I want—'

'Baby.' Grandma's voice was a little fierce. 'No nonsense. No one is fit for nonsense at the moment. Please don't be putting more bothers on us than we already have.'

There was a flurry of activity in the hall and Nonie came in. She kissed Grandma and then Harry, she came round the table and sat down beside me, she put her arms around me and hugged me tight. Mickey filled a plate with bacon, eggs, sausages and fried bread and put it in front of her, and Paddy poured her a large cup of coffee.

'Darlings, thank you so much. Poll, we've been missing you every second. The infants want you home pronto. Do you know what time I left home this morning?'

'Well, you're here. That's all that matters,' said Grandma.

'You should have come with us yesterday.'

'It was so sweet of you to think of it, but I needed my own car. We have to go home this evening.'

'We're going to stay for a few days. We can drive Polly back to Dublin.'

I didn't say a word.

'You may stay as long as you wish, but Polly must go home with her mother this evening. That is the last word on the subject. Eat up your breakfast. We have to be ready, booted and spurred, by half past ten. Harry will take Polly and me in his car and you two boys can take Nonie.'

'No sign of Sam?' asked Nonie.

Grandma said nothing. She put a large mouthful of breakfast into her mouth and chewed.

'He's a brat,' said Mickey. He looked at me and winked.

I wondered suddenly if he knew where Sam was; the thought made my face go red.

'You've all been brats in your day,' said Grandma, picking up the letters that lay around her plate and making her way to the door. 'We will leave at ten thirty.'

'Did I say something wrong?' asked Nonie.

'Mama is upset,' said Harry. 'As you might imagine. Very upset.'

'Yes. But I didn't mean to—'

'It's all right, Nonie; she'll be OK.'

'I bet you anything,' said Mickey, 'that Polly knows where he is.'

'I do not.'

'He writes to Polly. Doesn't he?'

'He does not.' I began to cry.

'Nonie told me.'

I was shocked. 'Nonie . . .'

She put her arms around me. 'I was worried. I just mentioned . . . and he promised . . .'

'You've read my letters. My private . . . Nonie! How could you?'

Harry took my hands and drew me up from my chair. 'Come on. This is all nonsense. Mickey, you're such a blithering tease. Leave her alone. We're all upset. Come on, darling Baby, go and clean yourself up or you'll never be ready by ten thirty. Lucky it's a funeral not a wedding so red eyes won't be noticed. I don't think any of us will mention this again, certainly not to Mama.' He pushed me gently towards the door.

Once out in the hall he let go of me. 'I don't know what is going on at all, but if you do know where Sam is, you must let me know. I will believe what you tell me. Maybe I shouldn't, but I will.'

We stood in the middle of the hall and stared at each other.

'I promise—'

'No, Polly, no promises, nothing like that. Just tell me the truth.'

'Well ... I have had a couple of letters from him, but they've been in envelopes written by other people, posted in other places, and they have never ... never said where he was. Never.'

'Inconsequential letters?'

'You could say that. Inconsequential.'

Harry sighed.

'I think he was going to Havana.'

'Havana? What on earth was he going there for?'

'He felt it was the place to be. He thought ... well ...'

'What did he think? The bloody fool.'

'That maybe they had found the way we should all live.'

Harry started to laugh. 'Bloody, bloody, bloody fool. Where did he get that notion?'

'Cambridge. I don't know. I ... He made me promise not to tell anyone. I ... Do you remember I went to Marcus's party?

He nodded.

'Well he was there, not actually at the party, but there. In the house. In my room.'

'But why you, Polly?'

I shook my head. He looked at me in silence for a while and then put his hand on my shoulder.

'It's all right. Don't worry. I think I understand. Here.' He handed me a handkerchief. 'Don't cry any more. You're not a baby any longer. None of us has noticed that. We won't say another word now. I'll sort it out after all this is over. I'll shut bloody Mickey up. I won't say a word to Mama. I'll speak to Nonie. Don't you worry, Poll. Run on up to your room and wash your funny face. Quick. We mustn't keep the domestic tyrant waiting.' He gave a strange little laugh and disappeared back into the dining room.

We all assembled in the hall at half past ten, plus Sadie in a long black coat, black hat and black gloves, a missal clasped firmly in her hand.

'The girls have it all under control,' she said to grandma. 'No need for me here.'

'But Sadie dear, you're not allowed.'

'For forty years I've looked after every one of ye and the Lord God wouldn't forgive me if I wasn't to be at the last burying rites of the master and I'll tell you something, I won't be offering it up as a sin when next I go to confession. It would be a sin not to go.'

Grandma looked doubtful, but Harry threw his arms around Sadie and gave her a smacking kiss on the cheek. 'Where would we be without you, Sadie?'

'Only God knows the answer to that.'

'I shall sit in the back of the car with Sadie and Polly can sit in front with Harry.' Arm in arm, Grandma and Sadie swept out through the winter garden and I scurried after them.

I only remember little images in my mind of the ceremony. I stood beside Grandma and I remember her face grey and unmoving. She stood through the whole proceedings, her eyes looking into the past she had lived with Grandpa, not seeing or hearing anything of what was going on around her. I remember seeing Dr Whelan at the back of the church and wondering whether Mrs Whelan knew he was there. Someone will tell her, I said to myself, and she'll eat the face off him. In the graveyard a north-east wind tweaked at our clothes and our hair and sent shivers through our bodies. The rector's surplice, well starched, crackled in the wind and

Grandma stood, surrounded by her three sons, on the very edge of the grave. She threw handful after handful of earth on the coffin, but never cried one tear. My eye was caught by a movement. The rector had closed his prayer book and was moving with outstretched hand towards Grandma when he came running up the little hill between the church and the graveyard, up which only fifteen minutes earlier the men had carried the coffin.

'Grandma . . .'

But she had seen him too and was off running to the best of her ability towards him. I thought she would fall, or one of her frail legs would break under her, but she reached him and he held her tight and safe. I longed to run and be held by him as well, but good sense prevailed and I moved closer to Harry and waited for them to come to us. Nonie took my arm.

'It's Sam.'

'Yes.'

'Did you know . . . ?'

'Of course she didn't know. Let her alone, Nonie. He's here and that's all that matters.' He took my arm and together we stepped forward to greet Sam.

He looked tired and rather nervous; his hair was uncombed and he hadn't shaved. He and Harry embraced; he waved to the other brothers and then turned and put his arms round me.

'Oh God, Baby.' His cheek was scratchy against mine. I was shaking. He held me for a moment, then he briefly kissed Nonie who was just behind me and returned to Grandma. He took her hand and kissed it, then drew it into the crook of his elbow and walked with her slowly to the edge of the grave. They stood in silence, looking down into the hole; there was no sound except for the cracking of the rector's surplice as the wind blew in hearty gusts. After what seemed like a very long time they moved over to the rector and the three of them walked slowly down the hill to where the cars were parked.

Later, after the people had all gone, we sat, lolling and depleted, in the drawing room, Sam beside me on a sofa, his head thrown back among the cushions, playing with my fingers with one hand, a glass of whisky in the other. The rest were scattered round the room, Paddy and Mickey, Harry and Nonie, and Grandma in the high-backed chair by the fire which crackled in the grate and from time to time spat glowing cinders out on to the rug. I remembered Grandpa's voice when he said that he didn't believe that Paddy Deery had any vested interest in burning the house to the ground and I gave a little gasp of laughter and Sam squeezed my fingers tight and we smiled at each other.

'Well.' Nonie jumped to her feet. 'We must be on our way. Come, Polly, run up and get your things.'

'No. No. You mustn't go.' Sam sounded distraught. 'Just one night. You can stay one night. Mama . . .'

'If Nonie has to go she has to go, Sam.'

'But Polly doesn't, does she? Polly can stay. I'll drive her up to Dublin.'

'Nonie says that Polly must go with her. Don't be tiresome, Sam, we're all a bit fraught and we don't need a row. Just shut up and leave things. Go on, Polly, go and get your things.'

'Polly!' He gripped my fingers so hard that I thought the bones might crack. With difficulty I pulled my hand free and stood; I ran across the room and upstairs. When I came down again Nonie and Grandma were waiting in the hall. Grandma put her arms round me and hugged me.

'Good, dear girl. Come soon again. Very soon. I am going to be a lonely old lady without my domestic tyrant. So I will be relying on you to keep me going. And Sadie, of course. She'll need you too.'

'Grandma . . .'

She squeezed my arm tight. 'Not a word. Do what your mother wants.' She moved away from me and I felt unbearably lonely as I watched her step back into her own life, somewhat imperious and totally alone. She watched us go out through the winter garden into the winter evening.

Sadie was standing by the car, a rug wrapped round her and a basket in her hands. She handed it to Nonie.

'A few little titbits for you to eat on the way. It's a long old journey, and there's some little buns for the children in the bottom.'

'You are so kind, Sadie.' Nonie opened the back door and put the basket on the seat. Sadie pulled me into a huge bear's hug.

'Come back soon, Baby dear, you'll be sorely missed so you will. Now off you go before I start bawling.'

It was a long time before Nonie spoke. We had driven through several trailing villages and the rain was bursting on the windscreen, making the wipers scream as they shoved the drops out of the way.

'Poor Beatrice,' was what she said and then she sighed, leaning her head forward the better to see out of the screen. I didn't bother to answer. After another few miles she spoke again.

'What's this with Sam? Tell me the Sam saga.'

'What saga? I don't know of any Sam saga.'

She sighed again, an exasperated noise. 'You can be such a pain in the neck.'

'You say saga. I say there is no saga. If you want a saga invent one for yourself. He is alive and kicking. You saw him. Why not a Mickey or a Paddy saga? You seem to think there is some mystery to do with Sam; if there is I don't know it. So leave me alone.' I pulled the rug up over my head and tried to pretend to myself that I was going to sleep.

I wished for sleep. Not just to stop Nonie trying to winkle out of me things I didn't want her to know, Sam things, Grandma things, Kildarragh things, but because I was dead tired and longed for sleep. Perhaps I thought that if I were to sleep, when I woke I would find that the last three days had just been a black, unhappy dream.

She was silent for a long time and I envisaged her face lit by the tiny dashboard lights, her eyes intent on the narrow winding road, avoiding when possible the potholes and the ruts made by tractors in their daily work.

'I know you're not asleep,' she said eventually. 'And there is just something I have to say. So I'm going to say it. I would like you to listen. I know you think I am unreasonable about Kildarragh and all that. I know you have some romantic notion in your head that they love you more than we do. It's just unlucky and very sad that Greg was killed, otherwise things would be different. We might be living there.' She gave a grim little laugh. 'I don't think that I would have loved that, but you never can tell. City person born and bred that I am. Anyway ... that's all supposition or whatever, the reality being that you're almost grown-up now. No more school after next term. College ... such fun, college ... that's when your education really begins and you start to make real friends. You grow up. I met your father when I was in college. Nineteen thirty-eight. We got married secretly, which seemed terribly romantic but infuriated Beatrice, because she would have liked all the panoply of a wedding. Geoffrey didn't give a damn about that but he hated anything to do with war, so when Greg joined up it was a furious sin in his eyes. But be all that as it may, this is where we are now, a different world, a different scheme of things, different characters to play our parts against. I'm happy. I am happy.' She banged her hand against the steering wheel. 'Yes. I am bloody well happy.'

There was another long silence. I wondered if she was crying, tears running down her face like the rain running down the windscreen. I decided that she was not. I decided that we had had enough tears for the time being . . . anyway, she was happy, she had said so herself. 'I am bloody well happy.' Her very words.

She drew over to the side of the road and stopped the car. She wound down her window and then fumbled in her bag and brought out her cigarettes and her lighter, which had belonged to my father and had his initials engraved on it.

'Let's see what's in Sadie's basket.' She pulled the rug from my head. 'Can you reach it, darling?'

I leant over the back of my seat and groped for the basket and she took a deep drag on her cigarette and then let the smoke trickle gently down through her nose.

'All right,' she said, waving the smoke towards the open window with her hand. 'There's no Sam saga. I'll accept that, but I don't like the way he looks at you.' She pulled a small strand of tobacco from the end of her tongue and flicked it out of the window.

Sadie had done us well; there were two plump chicken legs, carefully wrapped in greaseproof paper, hard-boiled eggs and a little parcel of salt to go with them, and a neat pile of roast beef sandwiches. There was a Thermos of coffee and two slices of chocolate cake.

'Are you listening to me?'

'Yes.' I offered her a chicken leg. She took it and laid it on the dashboard.

'Well, what do you have to say?'

'What can I say? I don't know what you're talking about.'

'Well you should. You must know the way men can look at women. You must have noticed. You don't go around with your eyes shut. I don't like the way that Sam looks at you.'

'He's my uncle.'

'And maybe that makes it worse . . . no, no, I take that back. I didn't say it.' She threw the remains of the cigarette out of the window. She also seemed to throw the remains of her words out of the window and became silent once more. She picked up the chicken leg and unwrapped it, looked at it for a moment or two and then took a bite.

'Mmm. What would they do without Sadie?'

I laughed. 'That's what everyone says.'

'I suppose that she and Beatrice will move into . . . well, perhaps Harry's house. Somewhere small, more suitable.'

'I wouldn't think so.'

'It would be sensible.'

'No one has ever accused Grandma of being sensible.'

'I suppose not. Is that a Thermos I see there? Pour me some coffee, please.'

We sat in the dark by the side of the road for about fifteen minutes, munching and sipping, then she threw the door open and shook crumbs and chicken bones and little bits of chocolate cake out on to the road. She started up the engine and sat for a moment with her hands quiet on the steering wheel.

'I would advise you not to see too much of Sam.'

The car moved off slowly.

'I don't really think I will be seeing anything of him, but thanks for your advice.'

'Sarcasm doesn't suit you.'

I pulled the rug over my head again.

✵   ✵   ✵

That is all there is, really. Not much of a story, I'm afraid. Just the slipping away of a house from its loving family, the breaking up of a family, not through any fault of their own, but circumstances, history you might say. Grandma stayed on at Kildarragh as I had known she would in her full health and strength for a year, and then she seemed to want to leave us. Well, maybe not leave us, but go and find something that she had lost. One morning she and I were sitting in her sewing room and she pricked her finger with the needle. She sat for a long time staring at the bubble of blood that balanced on the soft pad of her finger and I saw that she was crying.

'Grandma, what's the matter?'

'What will happen to Sadie when I go?'

'Where are you going? No. I don't mean that. You're not going anywhere. Not yet.'

She took my hand and kissed it gently. 'I'm going all right. Soon. You know, Baby dear, I don't want to stay here any longer. I love the boys and you but nothing's the same without my old Geoffrey. I'd like to go and look for him.' She laughed. 'He'd be so cross if he heard me say that. He didn't believe in the afterlife, as you know. No more do I. Out like a candle. I think I'd be better off out like a candle than hanging on here without the old man. I get mournful, dear child, and I don't like that. Anyway, I feel my time has almost come. Ever heard of a broken heart?'

'I thought that was only a figure of speech.'

'I thought so too. But now I know it's not. I worry about Sadie, though. I have left her some money, but that's not the point. Where will she go? Who will love her the way we do? These are important questions.'

'She has sisters all over the place, and nieces and nephews. There are lots of people who will welcome her with open arms. She might stay here and look after Harry.'

'Harry won't stay here. If that girl had married him I

think he might have, but they'll sell the house. The boys. They have no wish to live here, any of them; they'll go further afield, and Harry too. Grandpa thought at one time that he might leave the place to you, as Greg's daughter. There would have been some sense in that, but I can't do it, dear girl. They all need money and all the money there is is tied up in this place. Sam.' She shut her mouth after she had spoken his name, and was quiet. She raised her finger to her lips and licked away the spot of blood. I wondered if I should speak, but thought not. I felt it was better to remain silent. The wind tapped on the window pane and murmured words that only she could hear. She smiled briefly and put out a hand and touched my knee.

'When he comes back, you will be kind to him, won't you?'

'Yes, Grandma, I will.'

'That's all right then. Of course he may never come. He may have been right. Maybe that will be the place where people know how to live. I don't think so, somehow, but I could be wrong. I am tired, dear girl. Would you go and find Sadie for me? I think I will go to bed for a while.'

Her days grew shorter from then on until she was passing all her time in bed and would lie, propped by pillows, with her head turned towards the window as if she were watching and listening for something that none of the rest of us could hear or see.

On one of my visits to Kildarragh I asked her whether she wanted Dr Whelan to come and see her. She shook her head and whispered, 'Darling, he might have me up and about in no time. That's what doctors are supposed to do. I, however, wish to fade.' She paused for a moment and then whispered once more, 'I'm sorry that it is taking so long.'

It was over the Hallowe'en weekend that her wish was granted.

Children dressed as witches and devils roamed the countryside and knocked on doors asking for apples and nuts. Grandma had said that candles should be put in all the windows, so that the house would glow and flicker as the children came up the avenue in the dark. A memory, she thought, that they would hold in their minds for years. She died silently in her bed as they shuffled off down the steps, their hands filled with apples and chocolate bars, their heads filled with anticipation that on the walk back down the avenue they might hear the moans of the dead from behind the tall trees, they might be truly frightened, they might have something extraordinary to tell their parents. As I stood by the door watching the children disappearing into the night, Harry leant over the banisters and whispered my name. I closed the hall door and ran up the stairs. I followed him across the landing and into her room. She lay, pale as a peeled stick, her arms stretched by her sides, her face a study of complete content, her hair shining in the flickering light from the candles and the fire in the hearth. We stood hand in hand and stared down at her and I didn't want to cry, because her happiness was so evident.

✳   ✳   ✳

I waited for Sam for many years, but he never came or sent word. I searched for his face in the faces of men on the streets, in buses, trains and aeroplanes. I listened for the sound of his voice when I was in a room full of strangers. I scoured the papers for a mention of his name, alive or dead, but he was never written of among those young and handsome heroes. No one made headscarves with his face on them; he became no one's icon. I still wonder if he found Cuba to be his Promised Land. Anyway, after all these years what does it matter to anyone other than me? When push comes to shove in this busy and frightening world, who cares?

Now you can buy any of these other bestselling books
by **Jennifer Johnston** from your bookshop
or *direct from her publisher*.

FREE P&P AND UK DELIVERY

(Overseas and Ireland £3.50 per book)

Truth or Fiction	£7.99
Foolish Mortals	£7.99
Grace and Truth	£7.99
This is not a Novel	£7.99
The Gingerbread Woman	£7.99
Two Moons	£7.99
The Illusionist	£7.99
The Invisible Worm	£6.99
Fool's Sanctuary	£6.99
The Railway Station Man	£6.99
The Christmas Tree	£7.99
Shadows on our Skin	£7.99
The Gates	£6.99
The Captain and the Kings	£7.99

TO ORDER SIMPLY CALL THIS NUMBER

01235 400 414

or visit our website: www.headline.co.uk

Prices and availability subject to change without notice